sit,

stay,

love

sit,
stay,
love

j.j. howard

SCHOLASTIC INC.

Copyright © 2016 by Jennifer Howard

All rights reserved. Published by Scholastic Inc., *Publishers since 1920*. SCHOLASTIC and associated logos are trademarks and/or registered trademarks of Scholastic Inc.

The publisher does not have any control over and does not assume any responsibility for author or third-party websites or their content.

This book is a work of fiction. Names, characters, places, and incidents are either the product of the author's imagination or are used fictitiously, and any resemblance to actual persons, living or dead, business establishments, events, or locales is entirely coincidental.

ISBN 978-0-545-86157-1

10 9 8 7 6 5 4 3 2 1   16 17 18 19 20

Printed in the U.S.A.   40
First printing 2016

Book design by Yaffa Jaskoll

For N, C, B, M, G, and of course W.
You know who you are and what you do.
(Willow can't read this, but she
knows anyway.)

sit,
stay,
love

People vs. puppies

1. People complain. Puppies never do.

2. People can be sneaky mean. If a dog is mad he'll just bark, or maybe even bite. But there's no sneak.

3. People: not furry. Also, it's weird if they lick your hand.

4. They love you no matter what.

   (That one's all on the puppy side.)

1

The Closet Monster

It's really not all that hard to be invisible. I mean, first, don't talk. I haven't said anything at all in math class for the entire school year, for example. And that's why Mrs. Lawrence hasn't called on me one time.

Second, if at all possible, be plain looking. Have mousy brown hair and boring brown eyes and pale skin. Be medium height and medium size, too, if you can.

Third, hang out in a closet. But I'll get back to that.

It's not that I actually *recommend* being invisible. All I'm saying is it's pretty easy. At least for me.

I take after my dad for sure—my mom is the anti-invisible type. Her hair is very shiny and non-mousy, her eyes non-boring. Although, technically, she *is* invisible to me and Dad these days, since she left home last year.

But back to hanging out in a closet. It's my favorite place to be. My best friend, Melody, who was a genius (well, I'm sure she still *is* a genius, but since her family moved to Boston last year, I always think of her in the past tense), told me that I like closets because I'm a *chasmophile*, which is a lover of small spaces, nooks, and crannies. Mel loved big and unusual words.

My mother, who does not have any particular love of big words, just called me the Closet Monster. Mom always used the word *monster* to describe a person who was crazy about something: My dad used to be the Sports Monster, but later he became the Couch Monster. My mother was the Shopping Monster . . . mainly the Shoe Monster.

But me, I'm the Closet Monster. I'm actually more of a dog monster, because I am truly crazy about dogs. But my mother doesn't like anything that has hair or drools, so she always pretended that my love for animals was just a passing phase, which of course it wasn't.

But anyway, on the night of the fire, as usual, I was sitting in my closet.

I was making one of my lists, this one about why I preferred puppies to people. In my room, I had lots more lists, the most recent one being a list of reasons that I deserved to have a dog. I planned to present that list to the Couch Monster soon.

I'd been asking for a dog since about birth. And I have to say, I deserve one more than most people do. I volunteer almost every day after school at Orphan Paws, which is a dog shelter in my town. And if anybody has proved to be responsible enough to take care of a pet, it's totally me.

As I made the new list, I started thinking about how much more invisible I'd gotten since Mel had moved away. Once in a while it was sort of nice to be able to blend into the background. But most of the time it was just kind of lonely.

I was so lost in my own thoughts that I didn't smell the smoke at all. And with the closet door closed and my head-phones on, I didn't even hear the sirens.

My father forgot about me being a closet monster, so the very last place that the firefighters looked was the place where I actually was. I guess they had to go through the whole house twice. It was getting pretty smoky by the time a fireman yanked open the door, started yelling at me, threw me over his shoulder like a sack of potatoes, and hauled me down the stairs and out the front door.

I sat coughing on the front lawn, with most of our neighbors staring at me. My invisibility shield was definitely *off* at that moment.

"Where's my dad?" I asked the fireman who'd deposited me on the grass.

The man just glared at me and turned around and headed back toward our house. A few seconds later, a different fireman came out with his arm around my dad, supporting him. Dad's face was really red, and he was coughing even harder than I was.

I ran all the way up to him before realizing that I couldn't remember the last time we'd hugged. My dad just wasn't a hugging sort of guy. But right then he picked me up and squeezed me really tight.

And then a few seconds later he put me back down and started yelling at me.

"You almost gave me a heart attack! Where on earth were you hiding, Cecilia? Why didn't you come down when you heard the *sirens*?"

I stood there in shock. Between the stress of being hauled out of my nice, quiet hiding spot and thrown down onto the damp grass—and now being yelled at—I had to blink hard to keep from crying.

"I'm sorry," I said, putting my hands up as a sort of surrender. All I really wanted at that moment was for him not to be mad at me.

Dad's face softened. "I'm sorry, Cecilia. You just scared me to death. When I couldn't find you . . ." His voice trailed off, and then he enfolded me in another hug.

We stood watching the firefighters shoot great streams of water into our house for a while until one of them came over to talk to Dad. They walked a little away from me—far enough so that I couldn't hear what they were saying. When Dad finally walked back, he told me we were going to have to go to my aunt Pamela's house at least for the night.

Staying at Aunt Pamela's?

I'm not trying to be overdramatic here or anything, but it might have been better to just leave me in the closet.

2

I fall for every dog I meet but this time it's different

"Ceciliaaaaaaaaaa!"

As soon as I opened the back door at Orphan Paws, I heard Lori yelling my name.

Lori's the best. She runs the shelter on her own. And she inspires a lot of people to volunteer, but I suspect I just might be her favorite.

I knew I'd probably get extra points from Lori for showing up the morning after my house almost burned down, but the truth was, I'd been glad for the chance to escape before Aunt Pamela decided that she'd like to organize my Saturday for me.

Lori ambushed me in a hug right away. "Oh my goodness, everyone heard the sirens last night, and I just couldn't believe it when I found out it was *your* house! Are you okay?" She pulled away and gave me a once-over. "Is your father all right? How bad's the damage?"

"We're both fine. I don't know about the last part. We're staying at my aunt Pamela's." I frowned, thinking about how much I dreaded going back there in a few hours. "Dad said the firemen told him we're not allowed to go back in yet."

"Oh, I'm so sorry to hear that. But I *am* glad you're here. We've got a new little one who needs some TLC."

I heard a tiny whimper and turned around. Mitch, the vet tech from Dr. Mercer's office who came by to help out sometimes, was standing by the exam table. The whimper must have come from the brown blob that was sitting there, wrapped in a ratty pink blanket.

I took a step closer. There *was* a dog in there somewhere, under the dirt. He was an adorable pug, with an extra-wrinkly black face and matted light brown fur. There was a lot of drool. I spotted a smear of blood on the table, and my heart sank.

But then I made the biggest mistake ever. I looked that dog right in the eyes. And he looked back at me.

I've read about hearts melting, and it always sounded silly, but that's pretty much what it felt like. I took another step closer to the poor little guy, who hadn't stopped staring at me. Or drooling.

"Is he in bad shape?" I tore my eyes away from the little pup and looked up at Mitch.

He nodded sadly, and I felt my melted heart sink even further. "This little guy's been through the ringer. The county people found him behind a Dumpster over at the Super Saver. Looks like he was hit by a car. Whoever did it probably abandoned him there."

"People stink." The phrase burst out of me, and everyone nodded. Everybody who worked with rescue animals felt this way at some point.

"He's got a pair of cracked ribs, some lacerations . . . mange, obviously. And he's malnourished, severely dehydrated," Mitch explained.

"No collar or tags," Lori added, shaking her head. "If he was ever somebody's pet, they certainly didn't take very good care of him."

The little guy's eyes were still locked on mine. He was also still whimpering, just loud enough for me to hear. I took another step, and raised my hand to pet him.

"Cecilia, be careful. He's been growling when we . . ."

But Lori didn't finish, because I was already stroking his head, and he'd closed his eyes. The whimpering stopped. His fur was soft. He moved a little to scrunch closer to my hand, letting out a small noise of distress in the process.

"Who's a sweet little potato?" I cooed.

"Potato?" Lori echoed.

Mitch chuckled. "That's exactly what he looks like!" he said. "Poor little guy."

"I need to get to Winchester to pick up those donations." I looked up when I realized Lori was talking to me. "If I'm not there, Mrs. Frederick . . . well, you know how she is. And Mitch needs to get back to work. Could you look after him until I get back?"

I was already nodding. "But what about his ribs and stuff?" I asked both Lori and Mitch. I was good at cleaning up cuts and bruises, but I definitely didn't know how to fix serious medical problems.

"There's not much to be done for the ribs except to keep him still," Mitch told me. "And he seems to be pretty content right now." We all looked down. Potato's eyes were still closed, and he was snuggled in closer to my arm.

"Okay. His name's Potato, by the way," I announced.

"Of course it is." Lori smiled. "Thanks, Cecilia. We'll be back."

"Okay, see ya," I said, not looking up from the sweet little dog who was still nuzzled happily against me. I knew that since people rarely came in at this time of day, Lori trusted me to look after the shelter on my own.

I let Potato doze for a long time—almost an hour—and I sang to him. I often sang to the shelter dogs as long as I was sure nobody else could hear.

"Potato, Potato, you're the cutest puppy I've ever met, with a face no one can soon forget, and I love the time with you I've spent . . ."

I realized it was a really bad rhyme, but kept humming as I looked around the shelter, from the play area, which was littered with dog toys, to the exam table, where I currently stood with Potato. I could hear barks coming from the back of the shelter, which was where we kept most of the dogs. There were only two of them back there at this point—a cuddly chocolate Lab mix and a grumpy black puggle—and Lori had fed them before she left, so they were just playing around in their crates. It made me sad to think about dogs spending most of their time in such confined spaces, but Lori did a great job making them as cozy and comfortable as possible.

Finally, I decided that I should clean up little Potato. So, very carefully, I peeled away the ratty pink blanket and carried him to the doggy bathtub near the window. I then gave Potato the longest, slowest bath in the history of dog baths. I went super slowly to try to avoid him having to move much, like Mitch had said. I rinsed, and rinsed, and rinsed. It seemed like his fur would probably run out of dirt soon, but then there would be *more* dirt.

A lot of dogs won't look a human directly in the eye, especially rescued dogs. But not Potato. He kept staring into my eyes the whole time. He was trusting me not to hurt him, I thought. Which was pretty incredible, considering everything he'd just been through.

When the bath was over I gently patted him dry, grateful he had short fur rather than long hair. I went to work on his cuts, using cotton balls to clean them out with diluted peroxide, then dabbing on tiny blobs of antibacterial gel. His ear had been nicked somehow, and was ragged and torn. He cried a little when I patched it up, and I felt tears in my own eyes at causing him more pain.

When I'd done everything I could think of, I sat down on the floor and gingerly rested Potato in my lap. I held him and stroked him and told him about my life.

It would have been a short story, obviously, if I'd been talking to a human being. But I could tell a dog all the little things that nobody else wanted to hear. So I told him about eighth grade, from my worst class, which was algebra, to my best and favorite, which was history with Mr. Key, who always told stories and was nice to everyone. That was the only class where, on purpose, I sat in the middle of the room, rather than the back.

"My dad used to be a teacher," I told Potato, who only looked up at me when I stopped stroking his head. "He taught P.E. Can you believe that?"

Potato gave a little grunt, which I interpreted as agreement with my feelings about gym class.

"You get what I'm saying," I told him, scratching gently behind his ears. "P.E. *would* be my worst class, but eighth graders don't have to take it. Anyway, my dad stopped being a teacher because he'd been going to law school at night for about a hundred years, and he finally finished. So now he's a lawyer, but not the kind that makes a lot of money. But I think he likes to help people out . . ."

Potato kept listening patiently—happy that I continued to scratch his ears (and once in a while I kissed the soft fur on the top of his head). I felt like the little guy was particularly understanding when I talked about Melody moving away and how she was almost always too busy to Skype now since she'd joined the cheerleading team at her new school.

I was scratching his stomach, and Potato grunted happily. I ran out of words but kept sitting in the quiet shelter.

Another hour passed before Lori came bursting in the back door. She doesn't just enter a room, she bursts in. I like Lori a lot. She's in her thirties and always wears sparkly shoes and this bright red lipstick that would look ridiculous on me but totally works for her. Her parents started Orphan Paws, but she took over after they retired. From what Mitch has told me, Lori has added a lot of color and personality to the pet shelter since she took charge three years ago.

She looked down at the little dog in my lap. "You got him all cleaned up?"

I nodded. "Did the best I could. I wish I could take him home with me."

"I thought you weren't allowed back inside the house yet?"

"No, I mean, not *my* home. My aunt's allergic. I was just wishing."

Potato raised his head to look at me. He looked concerned, I thought. Like a little old man. A little old Mr. Potato Head. I rubbed his velvety ears and his expression changed to one of bliss.

"The other two quiet this whole time?" Lori asked.

"Yeah, not too bad. They barked a little, but they were mostly well-behaved."

Lori walked over to me and smiled down at Potato. "He's such a cute little guy. I guess I'll see you here tomorrow to visit him?"

I nodded. "For sure." Lori bent to gently pick up Potato from my lap.

It was hard to watch her put him into one of the crates where we keep the animals who are recovering, but I knew it had to be done. I wiped a stray tear out of the corner of my eye, then my eye kept watering because I think I got some dog hair in it.

I picked out the softest blanket and wrapped Potato up like a little burrito, and he let out an adorable puppy sigh and settled in, closing his eyes.

"Come on, kid," Lori said. "I'll give you a ride to your aunt's."

"Thanks, Lori."

I washed my hands, dried them, and put my backpack on. I walked back over to Potato's crate and, even though I'd *just* washed my hands, I couldn't help but scratch his head through the bars. He gave a little happy grunt and I could almost swear he smiled.

Lori called, "Ready, Cecilia?"

I nodded and whispered, "Good-bye, little Tater."

Seeing Potato all snuggled up in his blanket, I couldn't help but feel a surge of hope for him. And for the first time since the fire, I smiled for real.

Reasons Cecilia Murray should be allowed to have a dog

1. I have proved how responsible I am with dogs by volunteering at Orphan Paws for <u>8 whole months</u>.

2. I will ALWAYS walk & feed the dog. Dad will NEVER have to.

3. Dogs bark and warn about intruders = free house security. (Also, they bark when the house is on fire and the owner is in the closet.)

4. Since Melody left, I am alone. All the time.

5. I am better with dogs than with people.

3

Honestly, Cecilia

"Honestly, Cecilia," Aunt Pamela said, and then exhaled loudly.

Honestly, Cecilia is how she always starts off talking to me. If I'd gone to live with her when I was really little I'd probably think it was my name by now.

Aunt Pamela was driving me to school, so Dad could go talk to the firepeople again.

I sat back in the seat and tried to remind myself that living with Aunt Pam wasn't *all* bad. For one thing, she made the absolute best waffles. I couldn't remember the last time I'd had a fancy breakfast on a school morning.

My aunt is my dad's older sister. She's very protective of Dad, so she doesn't like it when I make his life less easy. Which, since I'm his *kid*, is pretty much every day.

"I just have to ask, Cecilia, what were you thinking, sitting up there in the dark . . . on the *floor*?" I snapped back out of my waffle coma to hear what my aunt was asking me. "You had an entire perfectly decent house to sit in, and you picked the *closet*? I just don't understand."

I thought about telling her that it wasn't dark in there . . . after all, I had a string of purple battery-operated LED lights. But it didn't seem like a terrific idea to tell my aunt that I not only hung out in my closet but I also *decorated* it.

"I'm *sorry* I didn't hear the sirens."

"Hmmph." Aunt Pam made a sound as she pulled up to a stoplight. Meanwhile, to make myself feel better, I thought about little Potato and the speedy recovery I was sure he was making over at Orphan Paws. I was so excited to see him again after school that day.

Aunt Pam looked over at me. "You know, we really need to

do something about all of this." She swept a hand up and down like she was Windexing a window or something.

"All of *what*?" I asked.

"Well." She stalled, but it was a very brief hesitation. "First, your clothes, obviously, though that may be up to your father. I'll speak to him. Second, there's your hair . . ."

"What's wrong with my hair?" I instinctively touched my straight brown hair.

"It's just . . . it needs more shape."

"Okay," I mumbled, crossing my arms and slouching down in the passenger seat. We were just two blocks from school, so I was sure she was about to run out of time to list *all* of my faults.

I gave a big sigh. "What else?"

"Excuse me?" Aunt Pam sputtered in surprise.

"I'm just saying, we might as well get it all over with," I said.

"Honestly, Cecilia—" she began, but I interrupted her.

"Why are we talking about the shape of my hair? My house almost burned down two days ago!" I felt bad talking back to Aunt Pam, but I was so frustrated I couldn't help it.

"Don't be overdramatic, Cecilia. The damage was confined to the kitchen and living room."

"That's half the house," I told her, sinking even lower into the car seat.

"Well, I suppose it is. But your father is meeting with the fire chief. I'm sure they'll let him know when it's safe to return. It will be quite a job cleaning up."

"Do they know what started it?" I asked, glad for once that I wasn't allowed to have candles in my room.

"Something electrical." Aunt Pam waved a hand dismissively. "It wasn't anyone's fault."

"But what about all my stuff?"

I hadn't let myself think too much about the contents of my room yet. At first I'd been embarrassed at having to be rescued, then I was just relieved that Dad was okay. After that I was dealing with the fact that I might have to stay with my aunt for an unknown length of time. Then after last night I'd mostly been thinking about Potato.

"I'm sure we'll be able to get your things soon," Aunt Pam said.

When she pulled up to the school, I sat up and grabbed my backpack from the floorboard. I opened the door. "Thanks for the ride," I said, leaping out of the car.

"You're welcome, Cecilia. When does your school day end? I'll pick you up right here."

"Thanks, but I'm working," I told her, accidentally slamming the car door in my haste.

"Cecilia, young ladies do *not* slam car doors. And what do you mean *working*? You have a job?"

"I mean, I'm volunteering. At the dog shelter. I told you all about it at Christmas, remember?"

"Your father knows about this?"

"Yup," I called over my shoulder, already jogging in hopes of not being late to science. I was also glad to be away from Aunt Pam.

I raced through the front lobby all the way to my locker, grabbed my books for the first few classes, slammed the door, turned, and ran right into something.

Or *someone*.

I fell backward, landing in a heap of papers and books. I

looked up to see that I'd bumped into Eric Chung, who was possibly the most popular boy in the eighth grade—with an attitude to prove it.

Of all people to run into!

Eric was already squatting down, gathering up some of the papers that had fallen all over the hallway.

"Hey, are you okay?" he asked.

"I'm fine!" I yelled. That is, I realized I'd yelled once I saw Eric frown at me, looking confused/horrified. Somehow, in trying to make up for being out of it, I'd overdone it with the volume.

Honestly, Cecilia, said a voice in my head.

Eric blinked. He handed me a stack of papers he'd gathered. "Here you go," he said, in a very cautious-sounding voice. Like maybe he thought I was going to yell again.

"I'm sorry," I said, fixing my eyes somewhere around the collar of his T-shirt. "For yelling, I mean. I just . . . I was . . . that is, I'm . . ." First the falling, then the yelling . . . I really just wanted to gather up the rest of my stuff and get out of there.

I looked up. Eric's very dark eyes were looking into mine. He actually seemed more concerned than frightened now. Maybe he wasn't quite as big a jerk as I'd always thought. He opened his mouth to speak again. I held my breath.

He spoke very slowly. "Uh, did you maybe hit your head or something?" he asked, in a tone that suggested that I had not only hit my head but maybe damaged my brain, too.

I let out the breath I'd been holding and closed my eyes. "No," I answered, deciding that nice Eric had probably been some sort of mirage. I scrambled to my feet, brushing the hallway dust off my jeans. I realized I had made us both late for first-period science. Eric turned and headed down the hall, and I hurried after him and into the classroom.

Mrs. Wilson glanced up from her podium in annoyance—it looked like everyone was already taking a quiz on the reading we'd done for homework. But then she saw it was perfect Eric walking in, and she smiled at him.

When she saw *me*, she started to say my name—no doubt to ask me where I thought I'd been for the first three minutes of class. But Eric stopped her by saying, "Cecilia was just helping me. I dropped my books." He zinged her with one of his I'm-so-awesome smiles.

Ugh, how annoying. The rules just didn't seem to apply to the Eric Chungs of the world.

After hesitating for a few seconds, Mrs. Wilson nodded, though she didn't exactly smile at me when she handed me my quiz.

I slid into my seat in the back of the room. Mrs. Wilson had a seating chart, but somehow I'd gotten the seat I would have picked anyway.

I started my quiz, and Eric, in the front, started his. His grade was probably going to be perfect, too. I realized then that in all the excitement of the fire and Potato and everything, I'd forgotten to read the homework chapters. So I made up answers and waited until Mrs. Wilson called for us to pass our papers up, drawing Potato's little scrunched-up face in the margin and wishing the day would go faster so I could go see him.

As soon as eighth period ended, I dashed over to Orphan Paws, even though it was raining and I'd forgotten my umbrella. I headed straight for Potato, but he wasn't in his crate. I felt an instant rush of panic. What if Lori had already adopted him out? He wasn't ready, I was sure. His cuts couldn't have healed that fast, and what about his ribs? If someone with little kids took him, they'd be sure to let him move around too much, and then . . .

I walked out the back door and onto the small patio. The sun was starting to break through the clouds, and the rain had stopped. I let out a relieved breath when I saw Potato sitting on the pavement, his leash tethered to a stake in the nearby grass. He saw me, too, and started to jump. I sat down beside him quickly so he wouldn't have to move too much. I picked him up and put him in my lap, lowering my head to kiss his soft ears, feeling happy for the first time all day.

After we sat in the watery sunshine for a long time, I picked him up and checked each of his injuries. I changed the bandage on his ear, and he licked my face while I tried to replace it with a fresh bandage. I was giggling and trying to avoid Potato's wet tongue when Lori came in.

"I see you found your patient," she said, smiling. She was holding a clipboard. "We just got in a new litter this morning.

Left outside a church down the block. Some kid gave us a tip-off."

"That's nice." I was gently brushing Potato's back, one of the few spots with no injuries.

"Cecilia! Five abandoned puppies isn't a 'that's nice' situation."

I frowned and looked up at her. "Not the abandoned part, of course. But puppies are always nice, is what I mean."

Lori sighed. "I suppose they are. Can you help me get them their shots? If you can tear yourself away from your buddy there for a few minutes, that is."

I petted Potato's head and laughed. "Of course. I can stay as long as you want. And we get out of school early on Wednesday, so I can totally help with the adoption fair."

"Oh, great!" Lori exclaimed. But in the next moment her expression changed. "Cecilia—I want to tell you something. I worry about you. When I was your age, I used to go to the mall with my friends on early-dismissal days—*not* help out at adoption fairs with old ladies."

I rolled my eyes. Lori was *far* from being an old lady and she knew it. But she had a point about hanging out with friends. I twirled one of Potato's ears, not looking up at her. I *used* to have someone to hang out with—Mel. But then she'd moved away.

I guessed Lori understood even though I didn't say anything. "Cecilia, when's the last time you talked to someone other than Mel?" she asked me.

My collision with the self-important Eric Chung floated through my brain. "It's been a while," I admitted.

Lori shook her head. "I know the animals are easier. But you can't go with them to the mall. You definitely can't take them to a dance."

"I really wish you could," I said wistfully.

Lori threw up her hands. "I give up. I'll bug you about this later. For now—puppies!" She headed back inside. I put Potato down and followed her.

For the rest of the afternoon, I snuck back to check on the Tater in between weighing and bathing and shot-giving for the new batch of adorable little gray-and-black mutts.

I'd planned ahead for when I had to leave Potato, with some chicken-flavored cookies in a plastic baggie. I broke two of them into smaller pieces and put them inside his crate to distract him while I left. I knew if I could give him a positive association to go along with my leaving that he'd handle it better.

Then, with Potato happily munching away, I headed out the back door of Orphan Paws, still thinking a little about what Lori had said.

4

Of or relating to turtles

The next day was Tuesday, and I missed going to Orphan Paws after school because I had to meet with my "team" to work on a project for our history class.

Allie Cross, the best student in our grade, and also one of the most popular, appointed herself the unspoken team leader. Allie had perfectly wavy blond hair, and rumor had it that she and Eric Chung had dated last year. Allie existed, along with Eric, his twin sister, Lily, and other good-looking guys and girls, in a social circle I could never imagine being a part of. Not that I wanted to be a part of it or anything.

Allie handed us all our assignments for the project, and I was supposed to write a section on the Dust Bowl. It didn't sound very fun, but I wasn't going to argue with Allie.

When I got home, I started researching the Dust Bowl online and actually kind of got sucked in by what I read. Then I was surprised to hear the little Skype sound. I scrambled to click ACCEPT, and a few seconds later there was Mel waving at me from across the miles.

I felt a rush of joy. It was great to see Mel again for the first time in what felt like forever. I missed how she always used big words—and her fashion sense. Not only could she pick the perfect clothes for her own petite, curly-haired self, she always helped me pick out the perfect shirt or earrings, too. Today she was wearing a sparkly blue top that made her eyes look an even brighter shade of blue.

"C!" she cried. "I miss you! How've you been?" she asked.

I told her the whole entire story of the fire, and she gasped and asked all the same questions everyone kept asking, which led to me explaining that it was something electrical, it was no one's fault, and I had no idea when I'd be going home.

"How could you not tell me any of this?" Mel asked, her voice going all high-pitched in her outrage.

"It *just* happened!" I told her.

"Well, you still should have called me."

And then again there was me explaining for the billionth time that I am practically the only kid in America without her own cell phone. "Besides," I added, "I had to go to O.P. to help out after school, and there was this dog there, and he's the cutest thing I've ever seen . . ."

"Cecilia!" Mel rolled her big eyes. "*Another* dog? You've got to get out into the world of people. You're turning into a hermit—not even calling your best friend when your house nearly burns down! You're getting positively chelonian."

"*Chelonian?*"

"Of or relating to turtles or tortoises," Mel recited. "Or in other words, *you*. Always crawling back into your shell where nothing can hurt you."

"Geez, that's very psychological. That fancy school might be ruining you."

Mel sniffed. "Not really. Compared to Pearson, everyone

here is so snooty! I can't go an entire day without someone scoffing at my PB&J, or asking whether or not I drink *coconut water*." Her nose wrinkled. "But anyway, I'm really sorry about your house and all." She leaned closer and whispered, "I know how your aunt drives you crazy."

I sighed. "Yeah, she's kind of a lot. But at least we have a place to stay, I guess."

Before I could continue, Mel started to look distracted, as if someone was talking to her offscreen. "I'm sorry, C—I've gotta go. My parents are taking me to cheer practice. The big game is coming up so we're nearly doubling our practice time."

"Okay," I said, trying not to look disappointed. "I really miss you," I added. My Skype sessions with Mel always felt way too short.

"I miss you, too, Turtle," Mel said.

Wednesday started out gray and cold, but by the time the early-release bell rang, the sun was shining.

I raced the few blocks to The Legible Lion, the little bookstore on Vine Street where Lori always had her adoption fairs.

Her best friend, Sally, owned the store, which sold used books, coffee, and really delicious baked goods. We used the little tables on the sidewalk to set up a few crates with the hopeful dogs, all cleaned up and groomed, in search of their forever homes. We had the gray-and-black puppies I took care of on Monday, along with the chocolate Lab mix and the black puggle. I was secretly glad that Lori had decided that Potato needed some more time with us before we tried to find him a home. He was at the shelter by himself at the moment, but Mitch promised he'd check in on him every hour or so while we were out. I suspected Lori was stalling adopting him out for me, in case my dad and I could go home soon (and in case after *that* I managed to get my dad to agree to let me have a dog).

There were also two fluffy white cats; Lori usually specialized in dogs, but sometimes she made exceptions for other animals. After all, we were both suckers for a cute creature—no matter what kind.

"Lori, have you ever had any turtles at the shelter?" I asked her, thinking of my conversation with Mel yesterday.

"What?" Lori looked up from the notebook she was writing

in. "Sorry! I'm just trying to work on the budget for next month. Would you mind going in and grabbing me an iced coffee from the café?" She handed me a five-dollar bill. "Get something for yourself, too!"

"Sure thing." I rose from the lawn chair I'd been sitting in. The street was nearly empty. Lori probably didn't even need me to help her today. I ordered an iced coffee for Lori and a lemonade for myself. As I waited for our drinks, I thought about sneaking back over to the shelter to spend some more time with Potato instead.

I walked back out into the sunshine and handed Lori her drink, then took a big sip of my lemonade. *Yum.*

A family—mom, dad, older girl, and little boy—had come by and they were asking Lori to show them one of the puppies. "I'll get one out," I told Lori, who smiled at me gratefully.

I slipped a harness onto the sweetest of the five puppies, a little gray fellow I liked to call Oreo. Lori always told me not to name the dogs, but I never listened. Even if I never said their names out loud, I still thought of them using the names I came up with. In addition to Oreo, the other four puppies at the fair were: Peaches, Twinkie, Mallomar, and Coconut ("Coco" for short). All in my head, of course. Clearly, I have a thing for food-themed names.

The little girl snuggled Oreo against her and squealed happily, but when it was her brother's turn, the boy recoiled in fear, even though Oreo was just wriggling playfully in excitement. And just like that, Oreo lost his chance at a family. They wandered off a few moments later. The mom thanked me, but the dad just looked relieved.

I held Oreo as I watched them go. No matter how many times I'd seen it happen, I still felt an ache for the poor orphan pup who'd just come so close to getting a home.

"I'm sorry, big guy," I told Oreo, kissing him on the top of his head and getting a big sloppy lick on my cheek in return. Instead of putting Oreo back in the big crate with his brothers and sisters, I carried him in and sat down inside the crate and let them all scramble over me. I giggled as all five tried to jump into my lap at the same time. I forgot all my troubles for a few minutes as I played with the puppies in the sunshine.

A shadow fell over us, and I looked up.

Eric Chung was looking down at me. I couldn't make out the expression on his face.

Ugh! What was *he* doing here?

I struggled to my feet, untangling myself from the pups, and crawled out of the crate.

Once I was back on my feet I realized that Eric was standing there with a lady who was probably his mom. And now that his face was no longer hidden in shadow I could tell that he was laughing at me.

Of course.

I stood up a little straighter. It really bothered me how superior Eric Chung was always acting. His family is super wealthy, and he never lets anyone forget it. He and Lily have these crazy fancy smartphones that are normally only available in Japan. And every time I see Eric use it at school during lunch, I swear I see a smug little smile on his face.

"Can we help you?" I asked him, a hint of annoyance in my voice. Lori looked up from her coffee in surprise at my tone.

Eric's grin faded a little. "We're looking for a dog."

"Why would you look *here*?" The words were out of my mouth before I could think. Everyone knew about the Chung family's dogs—there were a bunch of them, all famous for winning lots of dog shows. There were the two chow chows, who always won the biggest prizes. Then there were four other dogs—a Lab and three corgis. All purebred, of course, since non-purebreds aren't allowed to compete in dog shows. So it didn't make sense why they would come to Lori's adoption fair; I figured the Chungs only adopted fancy show-quality dogs, not strays off the street.

"Cecilia!" Lori frowned at me. "I'm sorry," she said to Eric and Mrs. Chung, who was petting the puggle on the head. "Please just let *me* know if you'd like to see any of these little guys out of their crate."

Mrs. Chung stood up. "Thank you," she said to Lori. "My son is looking for . . . a particular type of dog."

I gave a quiet scoff. *Particularly purebred*, I thought.

"I'm hoping to find a full-breed dog," Eric said to Lori, ignoring me. "I'm training one of our dogs for the next local show—the Winsted Winner's Circle. I'd like to try to prove to . . . some people . . ." He paused and looked at his mom. "I'd like to prove that an adopted stray could win just like the dogs we get from the fancy breeders."

Mrs. Chung rolled her eyes but smiled at her son. "I don't know where he gets these ideas," she said to Lori. She patted Eric's shoulder. "This one's crazy about animals, and he's such a big help to me, so I said he could try out this wild theory of his." She turned to Eric. "I don't see any dogs today that would fit what you're looking for. Maybe you could check back in a few weeks?"

Lori started to say, "We may have . . ." but then I shot her a warning look. "I'll keep a lookout for you—now that I know what you're looking for. I'll check in with Mary Carlton over in Winchester. It's a bigger shelter." She smiled at Eric. "It is always better to adopt than to buy. I must say I think your son has the right idea."

Mrs. Chung thanked Lori and started moving down the street. Eric nodded to Lori. He looked back at me for just a second before following his mom.

It was sort of weird how he was looking for a stray dog to

show, I thought as he walked away, but then I pushed the thought aside and started to help Lori pack up the dogs in her van. Eric probably just liked the *idea* of rescuing a stray. It wouldn't be long before his family was adopting another dog that cost more than a car and trotting it around a ring to win some fancy prize.

His mom had said he was crazy for animals, but a crazy-for-animals person wouldn't have passed up all seven of these adorable pups just so he could find the fanciest one to put on display.

I breathed a sigh of relief that Potato, the only purebred dog we had right now was safe and sound back at Orphan Paws. Not that Eric would have gone for him anyway: a poor pup with a torn ear who looked like, well, a potato. The image of Potato as a show dog was so funny I had to laugh out loud.

"What's so funny?" Lori asked me.

"Oh, nothing."

"Are you going to tell me why you were rude to that boy?"

"I wasn't! At least, I didn't mean to be. Not *exactly*, anyway. He goes to my school," I told her. "He's just sort of . . ." I trailed off. *Arrogant? Stuck-up?* "I just don't really like him, is the thing."

Lori stared at me for a few seconds. "Why do I feel like there's more to this story?"

"There isn't! He doesn't even know my name, I'll bet."

"If you say so," Lori said. She shut the back doors of the van. "Hop in and I'll give you a ride to your aunt's."

Lori cranked up the volume on her radio and we sang along the whole drive, so at least I didn't have to answer any more questions about Eric Chung.

Had I been rude to him? Eric *was* annoying, but what if he *had* wanted one of the dogs we had today and I changed his mind by being so harsh?

Maybe Mel was right. Maybe I was a turtle. Maybe all anyone could see of me was the hard shell on the outside.

I go by many names

1. Cecilia Louise Murray (my birth certificate; my father if I'm in trouble)

2. Chasmophile, chelonian, or whatever is on her Word of the Day calendar (Mel)

3. That girl over there (assorted kids in my class)

4. Honestly, Cecilia (Aunt Pamela)

5. Arf! (Potato)

5

There's no math in kickball

The next day I walked into third-period math class to find out that Mrs. Lawrence, who was pregnant, had her baby three weeks early. So she was going to be out for the rest of the year. Our sub was named Mr. Garret but he told us to call him Chip. After going over decimals for seven minutes, Chip asked the class if we wanted to start our homework or go outside to play kickball.

Of course all the loudmouths in the class yelled out "Kickball!" and started heading for the door.

"But there's no math in kickball," piped up Allie Cross. Lily Chung, Eric's twin sister, nodded her agreement.

But it was too late—Chip was already out the door. When I walked by Allie's seat she was angrily slamming her math book shut and muttering under her breath. I wasn't a fan of either math or kickball, but at least it wasn't very cold out, and this way I could put off the fun of fractions for a few more hours.

When I got outside, I stood in the back of the group as Chip divided us into teams. Then I headed straight to my usual position: the extreme outfield. I stood there for a few seconds, pretending the sun was much warmer than it actually was.

"This stinks, huh?" came a voice from somewhere behind me.

I jumped out of my skin, then whirled around. I'd really thought I was alone, based on the fact that I'd gone so far out I was almost playing kickball in a different school district.

The owner of the voice chuckled a little, but she ducked her head shyly at the same time. It was Lily Chung. I thought about how she and Eric didn't look that much alike: He was very tall, but Lily was very tiny. Lily had long, shiny black hair while

Eric's was short and spiky. Her skin was paler than Eric's, but that was probably because Eric was so athletic and spent a lot of time outdoors.

Lily was usually pretty quiet in class. But just like her brother, she was popular. It probably didn't hurt that their family had a lot of money and lived in a huge house with (so it was reported) a movie theater and a one-lane bowling alley.

"Can I hide out here with you?" Lily asked.

"Sure," I answered. I wondered if maybe Lily was just a little bit chelonian, too.

Lily let out a relieved sigh. "I just can't handle any more kickball. In gym class once, they made me play third base, and then the ball was coming toward me . . . Everyone was yelling, and then everything was bad . . ." She closed her eyes and shook her head. "Let's just say I wound up in the nurse's office with an ice pack on my nose."

I chuckled. "Sorry," I said. "I don't like it either. That's why I'm all the way out here—and I'm hoping nobody kicks one out this far."

I turned to look back at our tiny classmates kicking far off in the distance. Chip seemed to be showing the pitcher how to really do things right.

"You're not on any sports teams either, are you, Cecilia?" There was just a hint of hesitation as she said my name—like maybe she wasn't 100 percent sure that it *was* my name. Or maybe I was just imagining that.

"No—I'm garbage at sports. But I keep pretty busy working at Orphan Paws—the dog shelter."

"Your parents let you have a job? Wow!" Lily exclaimed.

"Well, I just volunteer," I said. I was surprised at how easy it was to talk to Lily—I realized I hadn't ever spoken more than a couple of words to her before.

"I have to help my mom with training sometimes. My mom is, like, obsessed with dog shows," Lily told me.

Of course. I was already familiar with the Chung family dog show legend. I thought it best not to mention the interaction I'd had with Eric and Mrs. Chung outside the bookstore.

"But that's really cool you have a job of your own already. Even if it is volunteering," Lily went on. "My brother would probably love it there. He helps my mom way more than I do. He's better with the dogs and everything."

We both heard Chip calling us back at that moment and started walking toward the rest of the class.

"Well, it was nice not playing kickball with you," I told her.

"You too!" Lily said brightly. She ran over to join her usual friends on the way into the school building. I watched her go. Maybe Lily wasn't as snobby as I thought she was. I couldn't say the same about her brother, though.

After school, I told Potato about Lily and math kickball as I brushed his fur gently.

When I'd gotten to Orphan Paws that day, of course right away I asked Lori how the Tater was doing. "He's still improving a little each day," she'd told me. "Although I must admit I think he does miss you while you're at school."

I'd smiled, feeling a warm glow. "Well, good."

"Your dad getting any closer to letting you have a pet?" Lori had prodded gently.

I knew why she was asking. She didn't keep any dogs forever.

And I knew that her husband had a strict policy about Lori not bringing home any more rescues from work. (They already had five dogs.) If I couldn't take Potato home with me, someone else would.

And I knew I couldn't.

"We're still living with my aunt," I'd told her, feeling miserable. The timing was really bad. But I knew I'd need to work up the nerve to talk to my dad about Potato. Maybe if he said yes to me having a dog after we moved back home, Lori would hold him for me. I figured I'd earned that much.

For the rest of the afternoon, though, I tried to put those fears out of my mind and just coo at little Potato. He seemed a little less skinny already—you couldn't count every rib. I fed him the little bits of hamburger I'd saved from lunch and he licked all the grease from my palm.

I fell asleep with Potato in my lap, and Lori had to wake us up.

He didn't even cry when I left—thanks to two more chicken cookies.

When I stepped outside I was surprised to see Aunt Pamela's blue Volkswagen waiting for me.

"What's going on?" I asked her.

"No emergency. I just came to pick you up. I thought I'd take you to . . . retrieve some of your things from the house."

"*Retrieve some of my things?*" I repeated, suspicious. "What's going on, Aunt Pam? Spill."

She frowned at me and shot me a sideways look as she put the car into gear. "Your father got the final word from the inspector today. The house is . . . that is to say, you won't be returning . . ."

"Aunt Pam!" I broke in. "Please just tell me what's going on."

"All right. But I'm afraid it's bad news. I'm sorry to have to tell you this, but the house has been condemned."

"What do you mean, *condemned*?" I said slowly, pronouncing each word carefully, like I'd just learned how to talk.

Aunt Pam kept her eyes firmly on the road ahead, even though we were approaching a red light. Finally, she turned to face me. "The fire department said there was just too much damage. They brought in a home inspector . . . and, well . . . it seems it would cost a lot more to bring it up to code than the property is actually worth."

My chest felt tight. It had been a small, old house, sure, but it was *our* house. And now it was all gone forever. My room. My closet. The spot on the stairway where I liked to sit and read and think about things. The little back porch, where Mel and I used to lounge in the summer, painting our toenails. All of it . . . gone.

"How . . . ?"

I guess I'd started to ask, *how could something like this happen?*—but I couldn't get the rest of the words out past the giant lump in my throat.

"Cecilia, it will all be okay. I promise. You know you and your father can stay with me for as long as you need to."

I knew she was telling the truth. But it wasn't a truth I wanted to hear. I just wanted to go home, and have the chance to bring Potato there, too.

Aunt Pam didn't have much to say after that. She drove me back to our old house, and I packed up as much as I could. Most everything in my room was wet or damp and covered in a layer of ash. Nothing had burned up, but it was pretty clear that a lot of my clothes were done for. Everything white or light-colored was definitely a loss.

Dad had gone to the pack-and-ship place to get boxes, and he came in the front door, shuffling his feet and looking defeated.

"Your aunt told you the news?" Dad asked me.

Part of me wanted to tell him that I wished he had been the one to tell me about the house. Somehow Dad always managed to get out of doing the hard stuff. But he looked so down I couldn't bring myself to say it. So I settled for saying, "Yes. I can't believe that's it—no more house."

"I'm so sorry, C." Dad's eyes met mine for just a moment before he turned and walked into his room. I took two boxes from the pile Dad had brought in and went back to my room to finish packing and clean up.

But first, I had to find the list of reasons I deserved a dog— the list I had been planning to show Dad. I found it lying on my desk, balled it in my fist, and threw it in the trash.

6

None of this is fair

I thought my week couldn't get any worse, but man, was I wrong.

I was sitting alone at lunch the next day when I felt a tap on my elbow. I turned around to see Eric Chung standing there with his tray. I choked on the sandwich I'd bitten into and Eric helpfully whacked me on the back.

"Are you okay?" he asked. Why was it that every time I saw Eric Chung he was having to check to see if I needed to go to the hospital?

I coughed and nodded. I had no idea why he was there when his popular friends were across the cafeteria. I tried to think of something to say.

"I played kickball with your sister yesterday," I finally told him.

"Kickball?" Eric looked confused.

"Yeah, we have math class together."

Eric still looked highly confused. "Okay."

"We were both in the outfield because we're not that sporty. I guess you guys aren't really that much alike."

Eric laughed. "You're right—we are pretty different." He paused, then added, "Hey, so I just wanted to tell you—my mom and I went by the shelter yesterday, and we found a dog to adopt."

"That's great," I started to say, and then a flash of fear went through me.

I heard him continue to talk, but now his voice sounded like it was coming from very far away.

"Yeah, we found the perfect dog—we even have a lead already on how we might be able to track down his papers.

He's a pug—I guess he's really been through a lot, but the lady who worked there said you'd been nursing him back to health."

Potato.

Eric Chung had adopted my dog.

It felt like I'd been punched in the stomach. It hurt to breathe. He was still talking, but I wasn't listening.

"Potato." I managed to get just the one word out.

"Yeah—that's the one! That's a cute name, did you give it to him? Of course he'll need a show name, but since he seems to respond to Potato, we'll probably keep it for his nickname. They said he needed some more recovery time but we could take him home next week."

"Hold on." My head was still spinning. I couldn't process this. "*You* adopted Potato?" I was standing up. For the first time in my life I really kind of wanted to smack somebody.

"That's what I've been telling you . . ." Eric sounded so calm. It made the whole thing worse somehow.

"He was supposed to . . . I was going to . . ."

But I couldn't finish the sentence. There was no getting around the fact that I was living with my allergic aunt. It didn't matter how much I wanted Potato to be *my* dog.

But oh, how I wanted that to be true. It was silly, but I had never felt such a strong connection with a pup before, and I knew that if I could, I'd give him the best home ever.

And of *all* the people to adopt him, did it have to be Eric Chung? It just wasn't fair. Potato wasn't cut out for show business. What if his dog-show preparations got in the way of his recovery?

Still, I knew that deep, *deep* down, I couldn't deny Potato a loving home. But I wasn't going to stick around for Eric to rub it in my face.

"I was hoping you could help with . . ." Eric started to say, but I turned on my heel and was already out the cafeteria doors before I could hear him finish.

I didn't know how substitute teacher Chip was getting away with it. But in math class he announced that we weren't even bothering with the seven-minute fractions charade today. No, we were headed right outside for more kickball.

Lily was absent that day, which left me alone in the outfield, fuming. I was relieved she wasn't there, actually. I would certainly have spilled out all my frustration about Eric and Potato and the dog show stuff, and she might not have taken to that so kindly.

Finally, the class ended and Chip called us back inside. I pulled myself together and put on my brave face, as my aunt always called it. My next class was history. I sat in the back (of course). Eric wasn't in class, just like Lily hadn't been in math/kickball.

Maybe they left early to go pick up Potato, I thought, before I realized that Eric had said they were taking him home next week.

I fought back another wave of sadness. I reminded myself that I was at least lucky enough to *know* the people who were adopting him.

Maybe if I could just get to know them well enough to ask for visitation rights, I would get a chance to see my Potato.

Lori had trouble meeting my eyes when I walked into Orphan Paws after school. "Good news!" she announced, in the most fake-cheerful voice I'd ever heard. "Your little guy there's got a forever home in his future."

I didn't say anything back, but bent down to let Potato out of his crate. I picked him up and took him with me into the back. I walked out the back door and sat down on a little bench.

Bending my head down close to his, I kissed the side of his face. He responded by licking the side of mine.

"I know you're disappointed . . ." Lori was standing in the doorway, this time using her real voice.

"Yeah."

"You know you're not allowed to have a dog, kid," she went on gently. "Unless something's changed? If so, I'll tell those people that . . ."

"No, there's been a change, but not a good one. We lost the house. It got condemned."

"Oh no! I'm so sorry—that's terrible! Does that mean you'll be staying with your aunt permanently, then?"

"I don't know. Maybe." I honestly had no idea. And Dad seemed so blue about the whole thing that I was afraid to even ask.

Coming over to sit down beside me, Lori sighed and reached over to pet Potato. He licked her nose. "I'm so sorry, Cecilia. But you know, the family does seem really nice."

I looked over at her. "Yeah, the boy—Eric—he told me today at school. I know the Chungs are taking Potato." I felt a spark of anger again. "They want to turn him into a show dog! Did you know that?"

Lori nodded. "Yeah, isn't that something? Potato here might go from being left out by a Dumpster to being a champion. Isn't life funny sometimes?"

I rolled my eyes. "Hysterical."

Lori patted Potato on the head again and went back inside.

I turned Potato around gently so that he could see my face. "You don't really want to be a show dog, do you?"

I could have sworn that Potato shook his head back and forth, just a little.

Eric Chung has everything

1. class president

2. frustratingly charming

3. rich

4. good at sports

5. my dog

7

Another dog monster

"Incoming!"

It was Monday—day three of math-class kickball. I yelled to give Lily a heads-up. Austin Fuller had kicked the ball incredibly hard and it was headed straight for us. We both ran *away* from the ball as fast as our legs would carry us, and the rest of the kids on our team all yelled angrily. Finally, Lily picked up the ball from the ground and threw it to Medi Banerjee, who was manning third base.

"You seem like you know what you're doing there," I told her.

Lily shrugged. "It's progress, I guess. I just wish I could stop running *away* when a ball comes flying at my head. I do it every time."

"Well, *I* think that sounds like a sensible thing to do," I told her.

Lily grinned. "It's not that I hate all sports. I really love skiing. And ice-skating. I just don't like . . ."

"Anything that involves stuff flying at your head," I finished for her.

"Exactly!" She grinned.

I was surprised at how much Lily and I had bonded over the last few math-kickball sessions. It was hard balancing how much I'd grown to like her with the fact that her family was about to take Potato away from me. I had managed not to mention anything about it to her, though. I liked getting to know Lily, and I was worried that bringing Potato into the mix would mess things up.

Chip yelled that class was over then, and we started walking back into the building.

"This kickball marathon's got to end eventually, right?" Lily asked as we made our way off the field.

I nodded, but honestly, I kind of didn't want it to. It was fun spending time with Lily. *You can always just ask her to hang out after school*, I could imagine Lori telling me. Hmmm. Maybe imaginary Lori was right. But what if asking Lily to hang out crossed some invisible social boundary? What if our maybe-friendship only existed on the kickball field?

"Well, I guess I'll see you later." Lily's voice pierced through my thoughts. She was already turning the corner to her next class, and I had to head the other way.

"Okay . . . Well, wait!" I said before she could walk away. "Are you doing anything after school, by any chance? I volunteer at Orphan Paws, and today I'm taking the dogs on a walk. Would you . . . would you like to join?" I braced myself for potential rejection.

"That sounds great!" Lily said with a grin. "I'll meet you at your locker after school."

And before I could even reply, she was already bouncing away.

Her brother may be a dog stealer, I couldn't help but think, *but Lily's not half bad.*

"Heel! HEEL! Why won't you heel?!" Lily shouted.

I cracked up watching Peaches, Twinkie, Mallomar, and Coco drag Lily around the grass. We were in the park across the street from Orphan Paws.

Oreo had found a forever home. But the other pups were still at the shelter. Now they were full of energy, having waited patiently all day for me to come take them out. Lily had volunteered to take the reins, which ultimately resulted in her crashed on the grass, tangled in a mess of puppies and leashes.

"I don't know how you do it," Lily said, slowly pulling at the leashes in an attempt to escape. We moved the tangle of puppies into the gated dog park. Then I helped Lily unclip all of the pups from their leashes so they could run around. "This is *exhausting.*"

"You get used to it," I said, sitting down on a bench. "Wait," I added, "doesn't your family have a lot of dogs?" *Show dogs,* I added silently.

Lily nodded as she sat down beside me. "But I kind of stay out of their way. Eric and my parents are the dog people in the family." She smiled. "I mean, don't get me wrong. Dogs are cute. But I think I'm more of a cat person."

I laughed. "Okay. I think I can accept that."

We sat there for a while, watching in comfortable silence as the puppies pranced around the park, chasing one another and playing with the other dogs. After a minute, Coco ran up to me and begged to be picked up. I lifted her up and she promptly started licking my face.

"You're just like my brother," Lily said with a grin. "He's crazy for dogs. And ever since he found a box of abandoned puppies outside a church last week and brought them to Orphan Paws, he's been obsessed with the idea of adopting a rescue dog. Our parents think that's a bad idea, but Eric wouldn't let it go, so they eventually gave in, on the condition he takes full responsibility for the pup. In fact, our family is gonna adopt . . ."

Her eyes flicked down and her words trailed off. I could tell that Eric had already filled her in on my relationship with their soon-to-be pup.

"Yeah, I heard about Potato," I said, trying and failing to suppress my immediate frown.

"You can still visit him, you know," Lily said softly.

"Yeah, maybe. But it's not the same," I replied, wishing we'd move on to another conversation topic. I didn't want to think about Potato and his new home right now.

"And Eric can be super annoying sometimes, but he's good at taking care of dogs. I think you guys would get along . . ."

"Doubtful," I said, standing up quickly and picking up the leashes. "But I am glad that you came today," I offered, realizing my tone may have sounded a bit harsh.

"Me too," Lily said. She stood up next to me, and together we gathered all the puppies and got their leashes back on.

As we headed out of the park, I thought about what Lily said about Eric, and how ridiculous it was. Eric might be a fellow dog monster, but that was no reason he had to take *my* dog.

But Potato's not technically mine, a voice in my head was quick to remind me. My confused thoughts followed me all the way back to the shelter.

"Thanks for inviting me," Lily told me.

"Sure," I said, and we waved good-bye.

8

Also, I smell like wet dog

The next day at school passed in a blur. I knew I didn't have much time left with Potato, so I was frantic to get back to Orphan Paws as soon as I could. The minute the final bell rang, I ran to O.P., threw open the door with my usual gusto, then leaned, panting against the doorframe.

"Was someone chasing you?" Lori asked.

"No." I paused for breath. "I just like making a dramatic entrance."

Lori shook her head, laughing. "Well, anyway, I'm glad to see you. We've got these two new guys in just now." She gestured to one of the intake crates, which held two very dirty medium-sized dogs. They both looked like mixed terriers. "I've got to go pick up some meds. Could you bathe them and do the flea dip?"

I nodded. "Sure. Whatever you need." I rolled up my sleeves and went over to the big sink to gather my supplies and prep. I glanced over at Potato, who was napping across the room, but I knew duty came first.

I gave each terrier a bath, followed by the dreaded flea dip. You had to apply the solution with a sponge just a little at a time, then towel the dog dry. The smell was pretty crummy, but hopefully it would work to get these puppies flea-free.

When I was finally done I took off the coverall I'd worn and washed my hands, then scooped up Potato. He'd woken up and barked happily at the sight of me. I sat on the floor with him and checked all his bandages—all his cuts had healed nicely, and he was moving better now. His ribs were probably healing, too, I thought.

I nuzzled my cheek against his. "Well, Potato," I whispered, "I know you've found a forever home. They are nice people—

well, I guess Lily is, and Mr. and Mrs. Chung. Eric maybe not so much. Except they *are* super into dog shows. I personally don't approve, Potato. I mean, with all the great dogs that are out there in every shelter, why do people have to *breed* dogs? It's very irresponsible."

I set him down gently and then walked a few paces away. "Come, Potato." I clapped my hands and he waddled back over to me. Then he stopped and looked at me expectantly, as if he were waiting for my next command. What a cutie.

"Sit," I said, motioning my hand down.

Potato sat.

"Can you shake my hand?" I asked him, putting my hand out.

Potato looked at my hand, tilting his head quizzically.

I gently lifted his paw and shook it, showing him what I wanted. Then I let his paw go and put my hand out again. The request seemed to register in his head, and Potato quickly lifted his paw for me to shake.

"Good Potato!" I said, elated that he'd listened to me.

Potato gave a small victory bark in reply.

"I'm going to miss you," I whispered sadly.

I heard a throat clearing behind me. "You're right. He really listens to you," said a voice.

I jumped a little in surprise. I never in a million years would have guessed who was standing there. Eric Chung.

"You scared me half to death!" I told him.

"Sorry. Just thought I'd come by and see Potato—see how he's doing." There was a look on his face that I couldn't quite read. I wondered how long he had been watching me, and if he had heard my rant about dog breeding.

"I don't think he's ready to go home with you yet," I heard myself saying, my tone harsher than I'd intended. I didn't stop to think—I just knew I wasn't ready to part with him yet.

Eric looked down at Potato. "He's a great example of his breed, build-wise. He'll be a fierce competitor in the dog show circuit."

I tried to hold my tongue, but I couldn't. "I don't think Potato's dog show material," I blurted. "I mean, I'm sure he'd be awesome because Potato can do anything. But he doesn't deserve to have such a high-pressure life. What if he doesn't perform up to your expectations? Will you be mean to him? Potato's been through enough, and he doesn't need any more stress." I knew I was rambling at this point, but I felt such a surge of emotion that I had to let it out.

Eric looked offended. "I'd never be mean to a dog, Cecilia, especially to one I'm responsible for."

"Well . . . good," I said, disappointed in myself that I couldn't come up with a better retort. An awkward pause followed.

Eric still looked a little miffed, but then moved closer to me and knelt down to scratch Potato's head. "There's a good boy," he said softly. Then, all of a sudden, Eric got up abruptly, his nose wrinkling as if he smelled something rank.

"What's wrong?" I asked. "I thought you came to see Potato." He'd moved a few feet away from where he'd just been kneeling.

"Nothing," Eric said quickly. "I—I just can't stay. But I'm glad Potato's doing so well. We can't wait to bring him home in a few days."

Before I knew it, Eric was out the door, and I was still sitting there confused.

"What was that about?" I asked Potato, who stared at me. The pup seemed to be thinking hard but had no answer.

I found out the real answer a half hour later, after I'd run home and slid into my spot at my aunt's dinner table. I hadn't bothered to change, since Aunt Pam had announced that she had made her famous macaroni and cheese.

Aunt Pam's nose wrinkled just as Eric's had. "What's that smell?"

"It's probably me. I guess I smell like wet dog."

"No, that's not it. I mean, yes—that, too. But you've smelled like that before."

Dad reached across the table to grab the bread basket. "That's flea dip smell, I'll bet."

I smacked my palm against my forehead. "Oh, gosh—yes. I totally forgot. That must be why he made that face! I smell like pyrethrin."

Aunt Pam was shaking her head. "Run up and take a shower and put on some fresh clothes. I'll warm up your dinner."

I frowned—the food did smell amazing. But Aunt Pam was right—the flea dip smell was mixing with it in a very unappetizing way.

I ran upstairs, almost tripping in my hunger-based haste. I rushed through a very hot shower. About halfway through changing my clothes it occurred to me that Eric Chung had caught me smelling like wet dog—and worse. But I didn't *actually* care what he thought about me.

Right?

9

Back to our regularly scheduled fractions

I slammed my locker door shut, giving myself a little pep talk. It was a new day, and I was pretty sure I smelled okay. Time to focus on the positive. Even kickball wouldn't be too bad, with Lily to talk to in the outfield.

"You ready for some kickball?" Lily fell into step beside me as we walked into math class.

"As long as we can hide in the outfield," I told her.

We took our seats but didn't get out our books, expecting the familiar call to go outside.

When Chip walked in I noticed he had on a tie for the first time since he'd started subbing for us. He also looked a little pale. Lily tapped me on the shoulder and pointed to the doorway, where the assistant principal, Mr. Danvers, was standing.

"Please open up your textbooks to chapter eleven," Chip said.

Austin Fuller started to yell, "Hey, what about kick . . ." but the look on Chip's face silenced him right away.

The rest of us shrugged and opened our books to chapter eleven. Lily and I exchanged a knowing look. I guessed that was the end of math-class kickball.

"And then I took the world's fastest shower. Because, well, you know how I feel about mac and cheese."

I was Skyping with Mel after school (finally) and had just given her the complete rundown of everything that had happened with Potato, finishing off with a recap of Eric running away from the stench of my flea-dipped clothes.

But even as I joked about my smelly encounter, Mel knew me too well to miss how devastated I was about losing Potato.

"There'll be other dogs, C! You guys get new dogs in at O.P., like, every single day. Soon enough, a new furry face will come along and you'll be in puppy love all over again."

I rolled my eyes, but I couldn't help but giggle. Mel always knew how to make me laugh.

"How's the living situation?" Mel asked. "Has it gotten any better with Aunt P?"

"It's been fine, I guess," I said with a shrug. "But I do hate to mooch off my aunt. A part of me wonders if my dad insists on staying here because he doesn't have enough money to find a new place." I felt a small weight lift from my shoulders. That had been a worry I had carried for a while, but this was the first time I had said it out loud.

Before I could continue, I heard my dad bellow, "Cecilia!"

"Noooo! I guess you have to go," Mel said. "But hang in there! Things will get better, I promise."

"Thanks," I sighed. "I hope. Talk to you soon."

I shut my laptop and walked the five steps out to the kitchen to see what he wanted.

"You bellowed?"

Dad smiled at my word choice, but it seemed like something was bothering him. "Your aunt has her book club tonight. I was *going* to heat up the rest of that soup she made for dinner, but then I just couldn't face it."

I made a face. "Good. Usually everything she makes is yummy, but I don't think soup is her thing."

Dad smiled again. "I think you may be right. Go get your coat."

"Where are we going?"

"Out for dinner."

"Awesome!" It had been a long time since my dad and I ate together, just the two of us. "Where?"

"Your pick," he said with a grin.

I thought about it for a second. "Can we go to Chili's?"

"Sure thing, kid." He turned and led the way out.

When we got there, we ordered plates and plates of food. My dad brought out a deck of cards, and we played a card game he had taught me when I was really little. I told him about Lily, and about how our substitute teacher, Chip, got busted for letting us play kickball during class. Several potato skins later, I was in a happy food coma. My happiness was cut short, however, as soon as it was time to settle the bill.

"I'm so sorry," I heard the waitress saying to my dad in a low voice. "Your card has been declined. Do you happen to have another one you could use?"

"Oh, of course," my dad said, his cheeks turning beet red. "Sorry about that." He dug through his wallet and passed the waitress another card.

"Is something wrong?" I asked Dad as the waitress walked away. I already knew the answer. I had watched enough TV shows to know what it meant when a card was *declined*. It meant we didn't have enough money to pay for our meal.

"Nothing at all, sweetheart," my dad replied. "There was probably just some mix-up at the bank. No need to worry." But it was clear from his expression that there was a need to worry. His brow was furrowed and his shoulders slouched.

The second card Dad gave the waitress thankfully went through, and soon we were on our way out.

We drove home in silence, but my mind was racing. It was

heartbreaking to see my dad so stressed out. I wished I could help him, but every time I tried to think of ways I could do that, I kept drawing a blank. *If only loving dogs could earn me money*, I thought.

Potato was due to be taken home by his new family the next day. So as we drove back to Aunt Pam's from dinner, I begged Dad to drop me off at the shelter and let me use my key to go in and visit Potato. Dad reluctantly agreed, but said he'd pick me up in an hour.

At night, with nobody else around, I found myself telling Potato everything again, and just like always, he was the perfect listener. I told him about dinner with Dad and fed him the bites of cheese I'd smuggled in a napkin inside my coat pocket.

"I still can't believe they're going to try to turn you into a show dog," I told Potato. He was moving more easily now, since his injuries were healing. He answered by rolling over onto his back and wriggling a little. When I didn't pet his stomach fast enough he even gave a tiny, indignant bark.

As I scratched his belly I thought about his future career. I shuddered to think of my little ugly-cute man prancing around a ring, being called a stupid name like Pinecone Happytoes McNally or something.

"Even if I can't adopt you," I told him, "I'm going to do my very best to save you from all of *that*."

Potato's favorite foods

1. Chicken-flavored cookies

2. Hamburger grease

3. Cheese (preferably in small chunks)

10

Thanks for the cactus?

Potato didn't seem to mind my tears, even though some of them were landing on top of his furry head.

Today was the day the Chungs were coming to get him.

Lori said she was going to let me have some time alone with him since they were coming around five to pick him up.

"Someday you'll get to have a dog of your own," Lori promised, putting her arm around me. Today she was wearing a white dress with gray French bulldogs all over it. I knew it was just my imagination, but I could have sworn the bulldogs were all staring at me with scrunchy-faced looks of sympathy.

"I don't want a dog. I want *this* dog," I said, sniffling and patting Potato's head.

She didn't say anything else, just nodded and disappeared into the back.

Potato and I were sitting on the floor as usual. I traced the little darker patches of fur above his eyes. I kissed the side of his face, where the fur was the softest. Potato looked into my eyes. He knew something was wrong.

How could I let him go?

The bell over the front door rang.

I looked up and saw Eric first. He was, randomly, holding a potted plant.

I felt immediately embarrassed; I was sure my eyes were puffy and red.

Eric's mom was with him. She was dressed in a very expensive-looking light-blue suit. She looked out of place in Orphan Paws.

Lori came out of the back, frowning. She whispered an apology to me as she took Potato from my arms and put him up on one of the exam tables. My heart sank. Lori started talking to Mrs.

Chung about how he'd been doing in his recovery and gave her some medicine. I stayed rooted to the floor, too miserable to move.

Eric bent down and held the potted plant out to me. Without thinking, I took it from him. When I looked down, I saw it was a cactus—one of those that sort of look like they're growing a brain on the top. I looked back up at him in confusion.

"I got it for you," he said. He wasn't quite meeting my eyes. "Sort of like a thank-you. For taking care of him and everything. I was going to get flowers, but then I remembered you said that cut flowers made you sad because they can't keep growing."

I stared at him, now completely confused. "When did I say that?" My voice came out a little shaky.

Eric stood up, still not meeting my eyes. He took the cactus from me, put it on a nearby exam table, then reached out a hand and pulled me to my feet.

"In science class last year, I think."

He remembered that? I felt my face redden, though I didn't know why. I looked over at the cactus, then back at Eric.

"Well, thanks," I said hollowly, as if the cactus in any way made up for him taking Potato away. My arms felt empty; I crossed them over my stomach.

"You can visit him, you know," Eric said, nodding toward Potato.

"Thanks," I said again. I was tempted to take him up on that offer *right now*, but I knew that it would be just plain weird to go to the Chungs' house for the express purpose of visiting a dog that never technically even belonged to me.

I looked over and saw that Lori was putting Potato into a crate for Mrs. Chung. I almost started tearing up again.

"No, Mom—I'll hold him," Eric said, going over to them.

I picked up my cactus and held the pot against my chest, maybe for something to do, maybe just so I wouldn't be standing there holding nothing.

Eric turned toward me, Potato in his arms. The little guy seemed happy enough there. "Do you want to say . . ."

I didn't let him finish the sentence. I shook my head, quickly muttered that I had to go, and ran to the back, still holding my cactus. I didn't want Eric or his mom to see me cry. I heard the front door bell chime again.

And then, a second later, I heard one sad cry from Potato when he realized he was going and I was staying.

"Where have you been?" Dad asked when he saw me walk into the living room at Aunt Pam's.

"I told you yesterday I was going to the shelter," I said, maybe a little meaner than I should have.

Dad blinked and I immediately felt bad. Things were awkward between us since the dinner at Chili's, and I promised myself that I would try my best to not make him feel any worse about our money/living situation—or feel worse about anything, really.

"I'm sorry," I said quickly. "I didn't mean to sound like that."

"What happened?"

"This dog I really . . . it doesn't matter." I knew it was no use burdening him with my drama, knowing all the other stuff he had to deal with.

"I know how important the shelter is to you, hon," Dad said softly. "I just don't want you missing out on spending time with kids your own age."

I sat down on the couch across from him. First Lori, then Mel, now Dad. Everyone seemed to have an opinion on my dog-loving, human-resisting ways. "I know," I sighed. "Lori and Mel said the same thing. I'll try to work on it." And really, I would try, I decided. Now that there was no Potato to visit every single day, my schedule felt more open.

"All right," Dad conceded as he heaved himself out of his chair. "Say, what's with the cactus?" I looked down in surprise to realize I was still clutching Eric Chung's guilt cactus.

"A boy gave it to me."

"A *boy*?" Dad's eyebrows went up.

"It's not like that!" I protested, hating that I was blushing *again*. "Trust me. I don't even like him. He's just someone who adopted the dog that . . ." I trailed off, worried that if I went into more details I'd start crying. "Anyway, it doesn't matter."

"If you say so," Dad said, giving me a look. He went upstairs to take a shower, and I went to my room to do my homework.

I put my earphones in, trying to distract myself from remembering Potato's last, sad little cry. And also from wondering about the cactus, and the boy who'd given it to me.

11

Not as bad as you think

Lily met me at my locker after school.

"Hey," she said, tossing her glossy black hair over one shoulder. "How have you been?"

"Okay," I said. It had been about a week since Potato had been adopted, and despite my plans to interact with people more, I had retreated into my turtle shell and was still spending most of my afternoons at Orphan Paws, meeting new pups and trying very hard not to love them too much. I'd also made a point not to ask Lily about Potato at school—even though I was so curious to know how he was doing, I was worried that if she told me any details, I'd burst into tears or something, or just get angry all over again.

"So," Lily went on brightly, "I don't miss kickball but I do miss hanging out with you on the field."

"Me too," I admitted, and felt my spirits lift a little.

"Apparently, it was Allie who complained to her parents about the kickball games, can you believe it?" Lily widened her eyes. "Austin and those guys are really mad. But of course they won't stay mad at her, since she's so pretty. Isn't that always the way it goes with guys?" She rolled her eyes. "But, oh my gosh, I'm sorry—I'm probably talking too much!"

"No, not at all!" I said, amused at her rambling. "I like people who talk a lot. My best friend, Mel, talks constantly."

"Oh—Melody Gray—I remember her. She was really nice. I mean—I'm sure she still is! She just moved, right?"

I nodded. Then, thinking of Mel, and of one of the fun things we used to do, I added, "Do you maybe want to come to Max's—the diner—with me after school sometime? They have really good milk shakes."

"Sure!" Lily didn't hesitate.

"Okay, well, how about today?" I asked. *You've got to get out into the world of people*, I could hear Mel telling me, rooting me on. My dad and Lori, too.

Lily's face fell. "I can't—I'm going to the basketball game." Then she smiled. "Hey—you should come with me!"

I'm sure my expression gave away my lack of enthusiasm for a basketball game before I had even opened my mouth. But Lily wasn't finished. "Oh, please come with, Cecilia! I always go, because of my brother, you know—but I sometimes get bored just sitting with my parents."

"All right," I told her, even though the idea of seeing more of Eric Chung was not appealing. "What time does it start?" Sports functions were definitely not my thing, but *my thing* seemed to consist of only caring for dogs and being a metaphorical turtle, so I figured it'd do me good to give this a try.

Lily squealed happily. "Yay! My mom's driving me to the game—we can pick you up. Say at six? You can text me your address."

"Sure. Except I don't actually have a phone."

"No worries," Lily said, pulling her own phone out of her pocket. "I'll just enter it in mine and then we'll be set."

"It's 411 Maple Street," I told her.

"Okay, see ya then!" Lily waved good-bye cheerfully and walked down the hallway.

I headed for the door, too, walking fast. I'd need to leave the shelter early to go to the game. *I'll have less time to spend with my Potato*, I thought, then realized that Potato wouldn't be there anyway. Sadness washed over me.

When I got to Orphan Paws, Mitch was minding the front desk.

"Hey, Mitch. Where's Lori?" I asked.

"She took a few puppies over to Dr. Prebble to get them checked out."

"Oh. Okay. Did she leave anything for me to do?"

Mitch shook his head. "No, she said you could have the day off. I believe her exact words were 'She needs to go be a kid for a change.'" He winked.

I laughed. "I'm actually going to a basketball game tonight with my friend Lily." It felt good to say the words *my friend*.

Mitch smiled. "Nice! Sounds fun."

"That remains to be seen," I said doubtfully.

Mrs. Chung picked me up in a shiny silver car. As I stepped out into Aunt Pam's driveway, I looked into the car's dark windows, trying to figure out if Eric was there, but it was just Lily. I felt a wave of relief.

Lily scrambled out of the passenger seat and joined me in the backseat.

"I'm so excited you're coming!" she said.

"I'm glad you're going with Lily, too, Cecilia," Mrs. Chung said from the front seat as she drove off. "Mr. Chung and I usually go, but we have a work function to go to tonight. We'll be there after the game to pick you up. Don't be late coming out to the parking lot after, Lily," she added, then smiled fondly at her daughter in the rearview mirror.

Lily giggled. "I am almost *always* late. It's a flaw."

I felt a little pang of sadness, seeing how close Lily and her mom were. And apparently, she and Eric were pretty tight, too. It made me think about my mom, and I wondered what she was up to now, in her new life without me and Dad.

We drove along toward the school, and then I couldn't hold the question back anymore.

"How's Potato?" I burst out.

Lily glanced at me. I wondered if she realized it was the first time I'd asked about the puppy all week.

"He's so cute," she said. "But Eric hasn't let me play with him."

"Well, Potato needs to rest so he's fully recovered in time to be trained for the show," Mrs. Chung explained, changing lanes.

Trained for the show. The words made my stomach clench.

"Oh," I said softly. I'd been right; asking about Potato, imagining him playing with Eric, was just making me feel even sadder.

"I'm really sorry you can't have pets where you live," Lily said. It sounded like she was picking her words carefully.

"Me too," I told her, swallowing past the lump in my throat. "You have no idea."

"Meanwhile, we're Pet Central," Lily said with a sigh. "We have seven dogs! It's so chaotic. All the barking!"

I laughed. "I don't mind some barking."

Mrs. Chung dropped us off at the school, and I told myself not to dwell on thoughts of Potato. I thanked Mrs. Chung for the ride, and then Lily and I walked into an almost-empty gym.

"Are we early?" I asked Lily.

"Just enough to get good seats," she answered.

"Is there really that much to see?" I asked.

"Well, there's the *game*," she said, sounding amused by my question. "I'm sure something will happen at halftime, too."

"Halftime? There's an intermission?" I looked at my watch, wondering what I'd gotten myself into.

Lily laughed, but not in a mocking way. "There's *halftime*. Intermission is for, like, Broadway shows." I laughed, too.

She sat down experimentally on a bleacher, then frowned and moved over a few feet. "This is good." Lily patted the bleacher beside her and I sat. "Have you seriously never been to a basketball game?"

I shook my head. "Not much for the sports, you know. I thought you hated them, too."

"Well, as long as I don't have to *participate*. We're strictly talking spectating here."

"It's still sports," I pointed out.

"Just give it a chance, Cecilia. It might not be as bad as you think."

"Okay." I realized I'd been sitting with my arms crossed, which I'd read online meant that I was being closed off. "I guess I've just been anti-sports since forever—my dad actually used to teach P.E. He tried really hard to make me athletic when I was little, and it was . . . let's just say the experiment failed."

Lily cocked her head to the side. "I can see where that would make you pretty anti. I think I can kind of understand. You know, being the twin sister of a basketball star . . . who runs away when balls fly toward her," she added, smiling.

"I guess you probably do get it," I said, smiling back.

People were starting to come into the gym, and I soon saw that a good chunk of our grade was walking in.

"So hey, Lily? Does *everybody* come to basketball games?"

"Pretty much."

"How did I not know that?"

She did that thoughtful head-tilt-pause of hers again. "I think maybe you've been in your own bubble, sort of. With the shelter and everything."

I realized in that moment that she was right. Lily Chung was surprisingly insightful.

I watched as Allie Cross and a gaggle of other popular girls sat down on the bleachers. They waved to Lily, and she waved back.

"Do you want to sit with them?" I asked, feeling a wave of dread. Lily still always sat with those girls at lunchtime and walked with them between classes. I assumed she must prefer to sit with them at games.

Lily shrugged. "It's okay." She dropped her voice and glanced at me. "Honestly, I could use a little break from them. I mean, they're my friends, yeah, but sometimes . . ." She trailed off, and then whispered, "They can be a little snobby."

I nodded, relieved that it wasn't just me (and Mel) who had observed that.

Lily flicked her hair out of her eyes. "It just gets a little annoying sometimes how Allie always has to be the queen bee, you know? And last year, she and Eric dated, so that was especially annoying."

Right. I glanced over at Allie, who was looking in her compact mirror and applying lip gloss. Why did I feel a flash of jealousy?

The bleachers were filling up fast, and the music that had been playing got louder. I realized the game was about to start.

The cheerleaders started running onto the floor. One of them did some kind of flip, and I held my breath, but she landed perfectly, her smile still in place. The whole group did a cheer and then ran off to the side. Two of the girls held up a big paper banner and the players started running in. The first one to bust through the paper was Eric Chung, and he did it with an energy that had everyone going wild.

The crowd was already on their feet and cheering him on, even though he hadn't actually done anything yet, except for breaking paper and waving his arms around some more.

"That's . . . quite an entrance your brother just made," I told Lily.

She rolled her eyes. "Yeah, he gets a pretty big head on game days," she said, smiling.

Along with the team, Eric started warming up—dribbling and shooting for the basket. But unlike the other players, he smiled up into the adoring crowd and waved.

Eric Chung could probably be the president of the United States someday, I decided.

"I mean, my brother is sweet," Lily was saying, "but sometimes it's just a tiny bit aggravating how he's so good at everything."

Eric Chung, sweet? I wanted to scoff. Instead, I said calmly, "I can see that."

"Being his twin can be tough," Lily added with a sigh.

"I can imagine," I told her, meaning it. I felt like I managed to disappoint my dad on a regular basis even *without* having a perfect sibling.

A buzzer sounded, and I jumped a little. I heard Lily giggle beside me. The game started, and Eric threw the ball and made a basket within the first few seconds. Almost everyone stood up (including me, since Lily was pulling me by the sleeve) and cheered loudly.

Between the loud music and the excitement of the crowd, I started to forget that I hated basketball. Right after Eric scored, a freakishly tall guy on the other team sank his own basket and the points were tied. The supertall kid and Eric seemed pretty evenly matched—the score kept going back to tied. This made the crowd even louder and more prone to stand up every time we scored.

Then Eric did something and there was a referee involved, and according to the Pearson crowd, what the referee did was wrong.

"What happened?" I asked Lily.

"They called Eric for traveling. But he wasn't!"

"Well, that stinks," I said, and Lily smiled at me.

The very tall visiting-team kid then got to make a free shot, and everyone on our side started making noise to distract him.

I joined in. Lily gave me a surprised look, then continued booing.

The kid missed and everyone cheered triumphantly. I didn't know much about sports, but I had a feeling that if my dad were there he'd have shaken his head and said something about bad sportsmanship. But the referee really *had* been wrong, so surely we were justified in distracting Tall Kid?

I sat back down on the bleacher. Wait. What was happening to me? Did I like watching sports now?

The music started again. "*Intermission*," Lily explained, grinning. I laughed.

The cheerleaders ran out into the middle of the floor and did a perfectly synchronized dance. I wondered then what it must be like to be so good at something everybody could see, that everybody liked. I mean, I gave a mean flea dip, but that would never be cause for applause.

The players were running back onto the court. Eric again looked into the crowd and waved at a few people. He ran right by us, and stopped when he saw Lily, giving her a big smile and a high five.

"Hi, Cecilia," he said, smiling at me, too, before running on.

Something about Eric saying hi to me made me feel less like an outsider who called halftime *intermission*. It also gave me a queasy feeling in my stomach that I couldn't quite interpret.

The rest of the game went by in a blur, with our team losing by just six points. I was surprised to actually feel disappointed. I watched Eric, along with the rest of the team, walk down the line and shake hands with the boys from the other school, who had won. Some of the guys from my school looked pretty angry, and they didn't seem very interested in shaking hands. But Eric smiled and gave each guy a firm handshake like he was already running in the election I predicted for him someday.

Lily and I waited while the gym cleared out. Mrs. Chung was driving the twins and me home after the game.

When Eric finally emerged from the locker room, freshly showered, Lily gave him a hug. He then turned to me.

"Thanks for coming, Cecilia," he said.

"It was fun! I'm sorry that you . . . I mean, I'm sorry that the team didn't win," I told him, cringing at my sudden inability to use words.

"It's okay. It was a close game."

"It was," I agreed. An awkward silence fell between us. "How's Potato?" I asked. Lily and Mrs. Chung had already updated me, but I needed something to make conversation.

"He's good," Eric replied. He left it at that, but his tone suggested he wanted to say more.

But before either of us could say another word, Lily interrupted, checking her phone. "Mom's waiting. We should go."

I followed the twins out to the parking lot and climbed into the backseat with Lily.

As Mrs. Chung drove, Lily told her about the game, with Eric adding a few details. I looked out the window at the dark and quiet town. Lily's words came back to me. She'd told me to give the game a chance, that it might not be as bad as I thought. And it wasn't. In fact, I think I actually had *fun*.

Was the same true for her brother? Maybe Eric wasn't as bad as I thought, I wondered as Mrs. Chung pulled up in front of Aunt Pam's house. Maybe I'd been wrong about more than just basketball.

If Eric was kind of a nice guy, all the better, I told myself as I waved good-bye to the twins and shut the car door. I didn't mind being wrong if it meant things were better for Potato. That was the only reason I cared anyway, wasn't it?

12

Do we have a deal?

"Hey! Cecilia! Wait up!"

I turned around when I heard my name. It was the next day, after school, and I was walking toward the doors, ready to head to Orphan Paws. I was sort of getting used to the ache of Potato not being there, but all those terrible feelings surged back as I saw Eric Chung jogging down the hall toward me.

"What's up?" I asked, watching as Eric put his hands on his knees, trying to catch his breath. "How long have you been following me?"

"A while," he panted, smiling. "I've been calling your name, but you didn't seem to hear me."

"Sorry." I looked down. *Here I go again with my chelonian ways*, I thought. *Now with an added dose of obliviousness!*

"Don't worry about it," Eric said, an unfamiliar shakiness in his voice. I was so used to his presidential charm and confidence that it disarmed me to see him so uncertain. "I—I have something I wanted to ask you." He bit his lip. "Can I walk you to wherever you're going?"

"Sure." We stepped out of the school together. "I'm headed that way," I said, pointing in the direction of Orphan Paws. We both started walking. "Is everything okay?" I added. My stomach dropped. Had something happened to Potato?

"Yeah." Eric nodded and ran a hand through his straight black hair. "It's just . . . well, as you know, I want to train Potato to be a show dog."

I nodded, biting back my tongue. I didn't want to argue with him again.

"And, well, Potato's proving to be"—Eric paused, as if searching for the right words—"a bit difficult to work with."

"Difficult how?" I asked, stopping dead in my tracks. Even though I knew it was none of my business, I felt protective of Potato and was ready to defend him against all snobby dog show trainers.

"For starters, he's very skittish," Eric explained, stopping next to me. "He won't really listen to anything I say. And I can barely make eye contact with him the few times that he comes out of his crate." There was a frustration in Eric's voice that I didn't recognize. "He just doesn't seem to like being around people, even though I've tried every single training technique in the book. So . . . so that's where I'd like for you to come in."

I looked at him silently, waiting for him to continue.

"I saw you playing with him at Orphan Paws. He listens to you more than anybody. And I was wondering . . ." His words trailed off.

"Yes?" I asked, my heart pounding.

"I was wondering if you'd be willing to help me train Potato," Eric finally blurted out. "And I know you don't like dog shows, and you probably don't even like me. But I really want to prove to my parents that rescued dogs are just as good as the expensive ones we buy from breeders. Potato is the key to my success." He paused to take a breath. "And you're the key to Potato."

My head spun. I desperately wanted to see Potato again, but the idea of "training" him for a dog show felt so wrong to me. I was about to explain just that to Eric, when he spoke again.

"Dog shows don't normally give huge cash prizes, but the regional one that's coming up is offering one hundred dollars to the first-place winner." Eric's eyes met mine. "If you help me, and if Potato wins, the money's yours." Eric's presidential charm seemed to have returned, but I could still see a little uncertainty behind his confident, hopeful smile.

I frowned. *One hundred dollars?* That changed things. I was torn. I did hate the idea of dog shows and everything they stood for. And one hundred dollars was far from enough to help my dad with our big financial concerns. But it might be enough to prove a point. This could still be my chance to help out my dad, even if in the form of a small dog-show prize. More important, I'd get to spend time with my Potato. And who knew? Maybe over the course of these training sessions, I could convince Eric that Potato just wasn't show dog material.

"So what do you think?" Eric's voice broke through my thoughts. "Do we have a deal?" He stuck out his hand.

I hesitated only a moment before I reached out and shook his hand. "Deal."

13

That word *we* again

Potato's training sessions were to begin on Saturday morning. Lily asked me to sleep over the night before. Dad gave me the okay. I was excited both by the prospect of escaping Aunt Pam's house for a night and seeing Potato even sooner. Also, since Mel had left, I hadn't experienced a single sleepover, so I was really looking forward to that.

Mr. Chung picked up me, Lily, and Eric after school in a shiny black car. He was wearing a fancy black suit and sunglasses. He kind of looked like a movie star.

"Hello, Cecilia," he said to me, and shook my hand like I was a grown-up. I tried not to stammer when I said hello back to him.

Eric got in the passenger seat, and I climbed into the backseat with Lily.

"I bet you can't wait to see Potato," Lily said.

I nodded. I didn't want Lily to think that I only wanted to hang out or come over to their house because I'd get to see Potato. It *was* a great bonus, but I'd want to be friends with Lily anyway.

As we drove away from the school, I felt a rush of nervousness. What if it was weird seeing Potato after all this time? What if he didn't remember me? And what if I then got so upset that I started crying, totally embarrassing myself in front of the Chungs?

I tried to push down my worries as we arrived at the Chung mansion. It seriously was a mansion—a huge white house surrounded by tall hedges. I tried not to gape.

Eric opened the front door, and a whole pack of dogs came rushing at us, barking happily. There were two chow chows, three corgis, and a chocolate Lab. Eric grabbed the collar of the biggest chow chow while Lily skirted out of the way.

I stood still, my heart pounding, as I finally spotted him in the pack, the tiniest of the bunch—Potato.

I shouldn't have worried. As soon as Potato spotted me, he bounded over, barking like crazy and jumping up to my knees. I felt a wave of relief and joy.

"Hey, buddy," I whispered. I sat down right there in the fancy foyer and held my arms out. But the chocolate Lab tried to fight his way onto my lap first.

"Sneakers!" Mr. Chung laughed. He grabbed the dog and pulled him away.

"Thank you!" I told Mr. Chung.

Then I gave Potato a huge hug. The little pup stood up on my legs and kissed my face very thoroughly.

"Guess he must have missed you," Eric said, looking down at us. If I didn't know better, I'd think Eric sounded jealous.

Potato crawled up into my lap just like we used to sit at Orphan Paws, and I kissed his soft ears. He turned around three or four times, making my lap into a bed, then let out a humungous puppy sigh and settled in.

I sighed happily as well and finally looked around. The foyer led into a huge living room with expensive-looking rugs and plush couches. Lily was now flopped on one of the couches, watching the dogs from a safe distance.

The two chow chows came up and sniffed me—one at each ear, but at Eric's whistle they sat down. The three corgis and the Lab now hung back politely. (*Can dogs be called polite?* I wondered). At Eric's whistle, they, too, sat at attention.

"What are their names?" I wondered out loud, rubbing Potato's head while he dozed in my lap.

"The corgis are Loki, Luna, and Baxter, and this little guy is Sneakers," Eric explained, patting the Lab on the head. "The chow chows are Scotty and Sulu." I wondered who the *Star Trek* fan in the family was.

"Nice to meet you guys," I said to the dogs, who were all still sitting. And I wouldn't have been surprised if they'd solemnly nodded in agreement.

Potato let out a loud snore, and I grinned down at him.

"Well," Lily said to me, springing off the couch and trotting over. "Now that you've been introduced to the canine members of the Chung family, do you want a tour of the house?"

"Sure," I said, although I was reluctant to let go of Potato.

Eric must have noticed my expression because he said, "Potato can come, too."

"Okay," I said, bouncing to my feet, with Potato still nestled in my arms. "So," I added, following Lily and Eric through the living room, "where is the bowling alley?"

"*Bowling alley?*" Lily burst out laughing. "We don't have a bowling alley." She led me through a large study, where Mr. and Mrs. Chung were each seated in front of sleek-looking computers. Mrs. Chung waved and called hello to me.

I frowned. "Really?" I asked, glancing from Lily to Eric. "I definitely heard a rumor that you had one. A private movie theater, too."

"I wish!" Eric laughed. "We do have a pool, though," he said, pointing out the large windows to a swimming pool in the backyard.

I sighed, thinking that I'd be glad just to have my plain old house back, even though it didn't definitely have a pool or a bowling alley. But it had been my home.

We walked by a cozy little room with a love seat, a big armchair, and a whole bunch of fluffy dog beds. Most of the other dogs were in there now, running around.

"That's the dogs' room," Eric explained. "They have the run of the house, but that's where they mostly hang out, especially when we're not here. That bed's Potato's," he said, pointing to a new-looking little tan-and-brown bed. It was oval shaped, and I swear it almost *looked* like a potato.

Potato had awakened, and he was squirming toward his bed. So I kissed the top of his head and reluctantly let him go, watching him trot off into the room. His tail wagged and his tongue hung out of one side of his mouth. I knew I'd come find him later.

"He looks really good," I said. I was really relieved but also kind of crushed that Potato seemed so comfortable here at the Chungs'.

"Yeah, he's been resting a lot," Eric said. "Mom got him a

bunch of special food that's good for his stomach and every-thing. But he was obviously happy to see you."

"I'm happy, too. Though it'll be hard to leave," I said, a sad-ness tinting my voice.

Eric looked uncomfortable. "Hey, I'm sorry—"

"Nothing to be sorry for!" I quickly said, turning around to follow Lily up the grand staircase. My interactions with Eric needed to be strictly professional, I decided. If we started dis-cussing what had happened with him taking away Potato, I'd get too upset.

Lily showed me the upstairs—her room was bright and dec-orated with floral wallpaper and pink rugs. She slept in a luxurious canopy bed, but the room was so big that there was an *additional* bed, a comfy-looking twin, in the corner.

"That's where you'll be sleeping, C," Lily explained, point-ing. I dropped my bag on the twin bed, and then Lily suggested we go downstairs and grab some snacks before dinner.

"See you at dinner," she told Eric as we passed by his room—which was next door to Lily's and just as big, but covered in posters of basketball stars. His shelves were lined with sports trophies, as well as—I swallowed hard—trophies from dog shows.

Eric paused outside his door and ran a hand through his hair. "Oh—um, I thought, maybe, well, I could go down and get snacks with you guys? And maybe we could play Uno or something?"

Lily groaned. "Seriously? You want to hang out with us? You always leave me and my friends alone!"

It might have been my imagination but Eric's cheeks seemed to turn red. "I was just offering to hang. But if you want me to hide in my room or something . . ."

"Okay, okay," Lily broke in. "Come on!" She started skipping down the stairs. Eric followed and I trailed behind, wondering why my stomach felt so funny.

In the gleaming kitchen, Eric and Lily greeted the cook, who was stirring a velvety-looking soup on the stove. *Fancy.* But I was glad when Lily pulled a jar of queso from the fridge and Eric grabbed chips from the pantry. At least their snacks weren't fancy. Just my style.

We ate the snacks in the den and played a few rounds of Uno, which was fun, even with Eric there. Then we had dinner in the formal dining room with Mr. and Mrs. Chung—tomato soup, roasted salmon with mashed potatoes, and mango sorbet for dessert, all of which was super yummy. Afterward, Mr. and Mrs. Chung went back to the study, and Lily, Eric, and I went to visit the dogs in the dog room.

My heart lifted again at the sight of Potato, who sprang off his dog bed and into my arms as soon as he saw me. The other dogs were sprawled on their beds, sleeping peacefully.

"Can—um, can Potato sleep with me tonight?" I ventured, hoping I wasn't pushing my luck.

"Sure," Eric and Lily said at the same time. *Whew.*

We climbed the stairs, me holding tight to Potato.

"Well, good night," Eric said to me, suddenly formal. "Training starts tomorrow morning."

Right. I nodded, my stomach falling. I'd forgotten about the training.

Eric went into his room, and I carried Potato into Lily's. Lily and I changed into our pajamas and then we watched a movie on her big TV before crawling into our respective beds. We lay there, talking about the movie we'd seen, and books we liked, and school.

The very best part was the little furry guy who curled up next to me and instantly fell asleep. It would be so hard to leave him tomorrow. I stroked Potato's head, and as I finally drifted off, I realized I'd never been so happy/sad before in my entire life.

Bright and early the next morning, both Potato and I gave Eric a look of disbelief as he showed us what he wanted the dog to do.

We were in the Chungs' backyard, where they had a little practice space. The weather had turned colder again. I shivered in my navy-blue coat.

Eric was running slowly around the edge of the little circle that was lightly painted on the grass. "See—this is what we want Potato to learn first," he said. "His gait needs to be even. He can't get distracted by anything—can't look around or break his stride. We have to practice a bunch so he'll be ready."

"Ready?" I asked, frowning. "Do you have him, like . . . enrolled in a show? Already? He's still recuperating."

"I know that," Eric said, sounding a little hurt. "We're start-ing slow. If he's ready, he can participate in the Winsted Winner's

Circle. That's not the one with the cash prize attached, but the show is a lot smaller and better for beginners. It'll be good practice for him. No pressure."

"Yeah, a name like Winsted Winner's Circle sounds super chill," I told him, rolling my eyes.

The small smile that seemed to be escaping from him surprised me. "Don't worry, Cecilia. We're starting small."

"Bye, guys!" Lily yelled from the front of the house, waving. She was leaving with her mom to go to her Saturday piano lesson.

I waved to Lily, then turned back to Eric and Potato.

"But what happens if he doesn't do it right? At the show, I mean." I picked Potato back up and pulled him tighter against me. Even though my ultimate plan was to get him out of show business, I still somehow hated the idea of him failing.

Eric shook his head. "He'll be fine, Cecilia. I promise. Again, this show is really low key. If he's ready in time, great— he'll get some practice. If not, that's okay, too. Besides, we still have a lot of work to do before we can go."

I'd definitely noticed him repeating *we*. "Before *we* go,"

I repeated. "Do you mean you'd want *me* to come to the actual show?"

Eric nodded. "I think Potato will do better if you're nearby. But if you don't want—"

I cut him off. "No . . . I'll go. I was just . . . never mind. Let's get started." I don't know why I was acting so strangely. I put Potato down on the ground and started walking around the circle. He followed me, as usual, but not in any kind of straight line. One of the Chungs' neighbors started running a leaf blower, and Potato jumped and stopped in his tracks every time the blower stopped and then started back up again.

"We have to teach him to ignore ambient noise," Eric said.

"Too bad we can't get him some puppy headphones," I joked.

Eric laughed. "That would be cool."

Again I was surprised by his response. Eric had a sense of humor?

"But since we can't actually do that—what *can* we do?" I asked. "What do you do with your other dogs?"

He pulled a bag of treats out of his pocket. "Positive reinforcement."

"Ooh, perfect. *Now* you have his attention." Potato had come running straight for us.

"The trick is to train him without turning him into a hefty puppy," Eric explained while Potato wagged his tail and jumped up, as if trying to reach the treats. "Good muscle tone is one of the most important elements of the judging."

"Well, this is just a regular Kobayashi Maru," I said.

Eric's head snapped up in surprise. "A what?"

"It's from that *Star Trek* movie . . . *Into Darkness*? It means a no-win situation."

"Yeah, I know what it means. I love that movie. I'm just surprised that you know it, too."

I gave him a look, offended by the assumption, then decided to dial back on the hostility. "I guess you're the one who named the chow chows?" I asked.

Eric nodded, grinning. "Scotty and Sulu! Most people don't get that."

"I didn't know you were a science fiction fan," I told him.

"I like *Star Trek* a lot. My uncle Miles always watched it with me when I was really young. He lives in Korea now, though, so I never see him."

"That stinks. I'm sorry." I hesitated, then added, "I don't really see my mom anymore. Although she doesn't live in Korea or anything. Just Buffalo, New York."

Eric was silent, and I wondered if I'd overshared about Mom. Potato was looking up at me with those big brown eyes, so I picked him up and got some slobbery kisses in return.

Eric cleared his throat. "Buffalo's not that far away," he said carefully. "She doesn't visit?"

"Nope. Not too often. Not this past year, anyway."

"That must be hard. Do you miss her?"

I kissed Potato on the top of his head. "Sometimes."

"That's too bad for your mom. She's really missing out on getting to know a pretty cool person."

I glanced over at Eric, startled by his words. My face felt warm. "Thanks." *Did he really mean that?*

"We should get back to work." Eric broke the silence. "We still have a ways to go with this little guy."

"Why Potato?" I burst out. Eric looked confused, so I added, "I mean, why is it so important to you to prove something with Potato?"

Eric seemed to be thinking about how to answer. "I grew up around dog shows. And it does kind of bother me—how it's all about breeding and pedigree. So I guess I figure if I'm going to do it, I might as well do it *my* way. And when I saw those dogs at the adoption fair a few weeks ago, it made me think about all the puppies out there that may never find a real home."

I nodded in agreement. *Are Eric and I actually on the same page about something? Other than* Star Trek, *that is?*

"I'd really like to prove to both my parents that a rescue dog can do well—maybe even win," Eric continued. "Potato might not have looked like much when he first came into Orphan Paws. But he's growing really strong, and he's the perfect example for his breed. If we can train him . . ."

"There's that word *we* again," I said. I was half joking, but Eric looked uncomfortable. He got all serious then, and we went back to training.

A busy hour passed. Eric started giving Potato a tiny bite of cookie whenever he managed to get partway around the circle without getting distracted. Finally, I stepped in, and Potato followed me around the *full* circle.

"He'll do pretty much anything for you," Eric said, sounding impressed.

"We bonded," I said, bending down to pet Potato's head. "Having a lot of treats helps, too. These chicken ones are his favorite."

"Good to know," Eric said. "Well, I guess we can take a break. You want some hot chocolate? My mom has this really good stuff she orders from, like, Europe."

"Do you have marshmallows?"

Eric laughed. "It sounds like marshmallows are a dealbreaker. Luckily, yeah, I think we have some."

"Well, then, I guess that would be okay," I teased him, scooping up Potato. "Don't worry—I'll sneak you one," I whispered to the pup. Marshmallows were definitely not on his show-dog diet.

"I heard that," Eric said without turning around.

As I followed Eric inside, I thought about the fact that sneaking Potato a marshmallow or two was hardly going to sabotage his show business career.

But did I *want* to sabotage it? What *did* I want? I wondered as I walked into the Chungs' house, my cheek against Potato's soft fur. The answer to that question was becoming less and less clear.

Show dog names: ideas

1. Sour Cream and Chive Potato Chips

2. Chicken Cookie Monster

3. Hufflepuff Bertie Bott's Sorting Hat (Lily's idea)

4. Captain James T. Kirk (Eric's)

5. Potato (mine)

14

Training a potato?

Dad let me stay over at Lily's one more night, so I left the Chung house early on Sunday morning. Parting with Potato was hard, and he didn't seem to want to leave my arms either as I walked toward the door with Mrs. Chung, who was driving me to Aunt Pam's. But at the same time, I had the hopeful feeling in my chest that I would be back. Eric said we still had a lot of ground to cover before the show.

When I walked in the front door, Aunt Pam was making pancakes.

"Good morning, Cecilia," she said primly. "Did you enjoy your sleepover?"

"I did," I said, which was mostly true—it had been a lot of fun sharing a room with Lily and, of course, getting snuggle time with Potato. But Eric still made me feel on edge. "Those smell good," I added, walking over to watch the batter sizzle in the pan.

"I thought I'd make them for your father today," she said.

I nodded as I set my backpack down. "He loves pancakes."

"It's also his birthday," Aunt Pam pointed out.

I could feel my face turning pink and my stomach dropped. *How had I forgotten Dad's birthday?*

"You forgot!" Aunt Pam hiss-whispered. "Honestly, Cecilia!"

I looked down sheepishly. "I did. I'm sorry. There's just been so much going on . . ."

Aunt Pam's face softened a little. "I know. You have had a lot of upheaval lately. I'll take you over to the mall this afternoon and you can get him a card and something to unwrap."

"Okay. Thanks, Aunt P."

She frowned a little, but nodded once. "Now why don't you come help me with the rest of breakfast?"

I washed my hands, still feeling guilty. She put me in charge of frying the sausages. I watched the patties carefully, trying to make up for forgetting about Dad's birthday. But they still got a little too brown on one side. I guess I had the burner on too high. Cooking was just not my strong suit.

"Is that sausage I smell?" Dad asked as he came downstairs. He was still wearing his PJs. Had he just woken up? I was starting to worry about him. He was taking the whole couch-and-sleep-monster thing to a new level lately. Not to mention the times I'd walked in on him stressing out over stacks of paper in the middle of the night.

"Happy birthday, Dad!" I cried, hoping it didn't sound too forced. "Sorry," I added, holding one sausage patty on my spatula at a time before transferring it to the little serving plate Aunt Pam had set out. "They're a little overcooked. But I tried."

"Makes no never mind to me, kiddo," Dad said with a small

smile. "Sausage is sausage. Thank you for helping your aunt." He took his usual place at the little round kitchen table.

I sat down beside him, trying to ignore the smell of burned sausage. Aunt Pam wrinkled her nose. "Where do you want to go for dinner tonight?" I asked Dad.

"Oh," Aunt Pam said. "I thought I'd make your father's favorite meal—meat loaf and twice-baked potatoes."

"I—I didn't know," I said, pouring maple syrup on my pancakes. "Dad and me just always . . . but, sorry—I didn't realize."

Dad jumped in. "What Cecilia means is that she and I always go out—the one with the birthday gets to pick the restaurant. Maybe we could go out tonight, and still have meat loaf tomorrow?" The look on his face reminded me—too late—about the Chili's incident, but I knew he wouldn't mention it now, especially in front of Aunt Pam.

Aunt Pam's face relaxed at the compromise. She liked it when things went according to plan—as long as it was *her* plan, that is. "That would be fine. Where would you like to go?"

"I'll have to think about that," Dad said, taking a huge bite of pancake. "After all, a birthday meal comes but once a year." Then he glanced at me. "How was the sleepover, C?"

I told him about the Chungs' house, and all their show dogs, and Potato.

"I'm glad you've made a new friend," Dad said. "Lily sounds very sweet."

"It doesn't hurt that her family is obviously very well-to-do," Aunt Pam put in.

"Seriously?" I snapped at her. "You think I should be friends with someone just because they're rich?"

"Honestly, Cecilia!" Aunt Pam exclaimed, her eyebrows going up at my tone.

"Cecilia, don't be rude to your aunt," Dad chimed in.

I felt my spirits sink. I felt bad enough for forgetting Dad's birthday, and now both he and Aunt Pam were ganging up on me.

"May I be excused?" I asked after I'd wolfed down my pancakes. Dad was helping himself to more sausage; I was glad he liked it despite the bad cooking.

"You may, kiddo," he said. "See you for dinner later."

Aunt Pam gave me a look. "I'll be ready to take you for those *school supplies* in an hour," she said pointedly, very obviously referring to our trip to get Dad's birthday gift. Aunt Pam would make a terrible spy.

"Sure thing." I put my dish in the sink, and then I grabbed my backpack and headed upstairs to my room.

I knew the room had once been my cousin Mandy's—it still had all the furniture that had been hers, and a lot of her old clothes were still in the closet (unfortunately, it was a closet too small to really hang out in). Mandy was all grown up now and working at a fashion magazine in New York City. There was also a Mandy shrine on the bookshelf in front of the window, containing all of her dance trophies and lots of pictures of her in high school. If only being coordinated and popular ran in the family.

I paced the floor, feeling restless in the small room that wasn't really mine. In fact, the whole house felt small after spending the weekend at the Chungs'. But I knew it was pointless to compare.

I sat down at the little desk, flipped open my laptop, and clicked to open Skype. I entered in Mel's Skype name and waited to see if she would pick up. When she didn't, I walked over to the bed and sat down, zipping open the backpack I'd taken to Lily's. I thought about how sad I'd felt the first time I'd tried to Skype Mel, after she'd moved, when she didn't answer. I'd felt so alone. But now, even though I still missed her and wanted to talk to her, at least I didn't feel so bad.

I heard the Skype call sound and almost tripped over my sneakers on my way back to the desk. Mel was calling me back!

"Hey, stranger!" I said as her image appeared on the screen.

"Hey yourself!" Mel smiled. The Internet at Aunt Pam's house was spotty, and it didn't help that the computer was old. It seemed to be a particularly bad connection today, because Mel kept freezing or dissolving into little pixels. But it was still good to see her. She was wearing a bright purple T-shirt with a sparkly black megaphone on it that said CHEER. A matching purple headband kept her curly hair pulled back from her face.

"You holding up okay?" Mel asked. "Last time we talked you were really stressed out about your dad."

"Yeah, it's gotten worse, actually . . ." I went on to tell her about our awkward night at Chili's and how Dad seemed down in the dumps in general, worrying about money. "And now I've struck a deal with Eric Chung so I could maybe earn some cash to help Dad out a little . . ."

Mel raised an eyebrow, and then her image froze that way for a while. I wished I knew how to take a screenshot on this computer, because it was a really funny face. "Wait. You mean *the* Eric Chung—basketball star, student council vice president?" Mel's voice asked, though her image stayed frozen.

"Yes—the Eric Chung. And he's the *president* of our class this year."

"I'm not surprised. Is he still a show-off? And why are you *helping* him?"

I didn't really know how to answer that. There were too many things to explain. "I've gotten to know his sister—you remember, Lily?" Mel's image unfroze and nodded. "She's really nice. Eric is totally arrogant, though. I mean, at least he seems that way at first . . ."

"Aha. So he's improving on closer acquaintance. Very interesting." Mel winked.

"It's *not* interesting. I'm just helping him to train Potato."

Mel's face got bigger in my screen as she leaned forward. "You're what? *Training a potato?* This connection stinks."

I laughed. "Remember? The dog's name is Potato," I said. "Eric wants to enter him in a dog show. Potato listens to me, so I'm helping Eric train him."

Mel looked confused. "I thought you hated dog shows."

"I still do. Why breed dogs when there are so many that need homes out there?"

"Pretty sure I've heard this speech." Mel rolled her eyes and grinned. "So what's changed?"

I opened my mouth to say *nothing*, but I realized that wasn't true. *Potato* was what had changed. I didn't know yet if he'd take to dog-show life, but what if he did? And if Eric kept asking me to help train him, I could still see him.

"I haven't actually been to any of the shows yet," I finally told Mel. "I guess I'm going to decide for sure how I feel when we go to the first one next weekend."

"Cecilia Murray—reserving judgment? Very uncharacteristic."

It was my turn to roll my eyes at Mel. "You and your giant words. Have you been reading the thesaurus for fun again?"

She stuck her tongue out at me, and I laughed when the image froze again. "No, but I've been reading *lots* of other books. Oh, hang on." She paused and looked at something offscreen. "C, I've got to go—my dad's waiting in the car. I'll talk to you later, 'kay?" With that, she hit the disconnect button, and the pixelated image of her vanished.

"Bye, Mel," I said to the empty blue screen. I had about half an hour before Aunt Pam would take me to the mall, so I closed the laptop and went back to my math homework.

I thought back to Mel's comment about reserving judgment. Was I really that quick to hate things? The question hung in my mind until I heard Aunt Pam calling me from downstairs.

15

Maybe not, then

Lily passed me a small bowl of food and I looked down at it in confusion. "It's kimchi," she whispered. "It's basically cabbage, just crunchier and spicier."

"Does it taste good?" I asked hesitantly.

She giggled. "Yes, I promise."

I spooned a little of the red, leafy stuff onto my plate and took an experimental bite. The flavor was strong and surprising, but I didn't hate it. In fact, it was pretty delicious. I spooned some more onto my plate, along with brown rice and a bunch of other pickled vegetables. At the center of the table was a large pot of soup—an orange-red broth filled with tofu and veggie dumplings—and Mr. Chung was busy scooping it into individual bowls for us. Their chef was off for the night, so Mr. Chung had done the cooking, and I was impressed by how good it all looked.

I'd never had Korean food before, and it was very different from what I was used to. My dad was a master of only one dish—frozen pizza. My aunt was an awesome cook, but everything she made was either deep-fried or filled with cheese. It was nice to try something new.

It was Wednesday night—Eric had asked me to come help him get Potato ready for the Winner's Circle show on Saturday. Mrs. Chung was at a work event, so it was just Mr. Chung, Eric, Lily, and me (well, and about five dogs under our feet). Sadly, Potato had switched allegiances, at least during dinner. Lily was the one who always snuck him a bite of food under the table, so it was *her* feet he sat on during meals. I wondered if Potato liked kimchi, too.

"Hey, Cecilia, I've got good news. We can do the rally *and* the show now on Saturday," Eric announced. "I got Potato's papers in the mail yesterday."

Eric had explained to me that the rally part of the show was a little obstacle course, and it was open to all dogs. But for the traditional dog show part your dog needed to be purebred and have papers.

"How is that even possible?" I asked around a mouthful of food. "Potato was found beside a Dumpster at a grocery store. If somebody bothered to register him and stuff, how did he end up *there*?"

Eric shook his head sadly. "I don't know. But he was born in Hartford, and his parents were both pedigree, from the same breeder."

"How can you be sure it's him?" I asked, peeking under the table to see Potato munching away happily beside Lily's feet.

"My mom's got a guy who investigates this kind of thing," Eric explained. "Besides, Potato's still got his microchip, so it's easy to prove his identity."

I shook my head. "Proving the identity of a dog. What kind of person even does that for a living? Is he like a doggy private detective?"

Lily giggled. "That sounds like a cartoon that would be on the Disney Channel."

I couldn't help laughing, too.

Eric, of course, stayed serious. "He wasn't registered with a show name, just a nickname. So we need to come up with one of those. I had one idea—we could put both our last names in, and also a shout-out to the name you gave him. How about Murray Chung Fried Potatoes?" He smiled and picked up his glass of water to take a drink.

Lily burst out with a laugh. "Seriously? That sounds like you guys are married . . . and your kids are French fries."

Eric choked and sprayed water across the table, mostly onto his sister. Then Mr. Chung burst out laughing. I laughed, too, even if I felt myself blushing at the idea of me and Eric being *married*. Too weird. Eric's face was red, too. Lily was wiping her face with a napkin, and Potato was trying to climb my legs to get a better view of all the action.

"Maybe not, then," Eric finally said, and Lily stopped glaring at him about the water spray and started laughing again.

I had to put my head down to keep from grinning. I concentrated on my soup while Mr. Chung told the twins about some trip they were taking over the summer.

I didn't meet Eric's eyes for the rest of dinner. When we stood up to leave the table he still looked a little embarrassed at the name he'd come up with—and Lily's take on it.

After dinner, we let Potato practice his circle run for a few minutes in the yard, but when it got dark we headed inside. "Can you come back tomorrow?" Eric asked.

"I really have to go to Orphan Paws," I told him. "I usually go every day. Lori left a message on the machine at my aunt's house yesterday to say she's really behind."

Eric stopped walking. "I'm sorry—I've been taking up all your time with this project."

I shrugged. "I like helping with Potato. But I can't leave Lori hanging."

"Does she need more volunteers?"

"Yeah, we pretty much always need more help."

"What if I helped tomorrow, and then we could both work with Potato on Friday right before the show?"

I almost tripped I was so surprised. *Eric, helping at the pet shelter?* "Well . . . yeah, I guess that'd be okay. I mean, it'd be good. Lori would be really happy."

And she'll probably squeal and ask you a million questions if you bring a boy with you to O.P., said a little voice in my head, but I did my best to ignore it.

"So we can walk there from school, right?" Eric was asking. "I could meet you after last period—at your locker?" I nodded. "Okay, see you tomorrow," he said. "Thanks again." He waved and headed up the stairs.

I looked down at Potato, who was looking up at me, seeming for all the world as though he'd understood our conversation.

"I know, weird, right?" I said to him.

"Yeah, it *is* a little weird how you talk to him like he's a person." Lily appeared from the kitchen and made me jump. "But it's also really sweet."

I laughed, flustered but not embarrassed. "Your brother is going to volunteer with me at Orphan Paws tomorrow," I explained to Lily.

"Oh! That *is* kind of weird," she said. "But *nothing's* beating that name idea of his!" she sang. "Never getting over that."

"Me neither," I said, bending down to kiss Potato good-bye.

"I brought a friend to help today," I told Lori as I stepped into Orphan Paws, with Eric right behind me. "This is Eric. Do you remember he and his mom adopted—"

"Potato—of course. You're the dog-show folks." Lori smiled at Eric but then turned to me and gave a look that very clearly said, *I will have a bajillion questions for you once this boy leaves.* Today she was wearing jeans and a blue shirt with WHO LET THE DOGS OUT? printed on it in bright pink letters.

Eric nodded at Lori. "Nice to see you again. I hope it's okay that Cecilia brought me? She's been helping me train Potato, and she said you guys were backed up here."

"It's more than okay!" Lori said, already digging through a

pile of aprons to find one for Eric. She found one and tossed it to him. "So here's the intake area . . ." She started giving him the speed tour.

I worked on reorganizing the most recent intake files while Lori showed Eric around. Lori usually moved too fast to really keep the files straight—so she kept things in a pile until I came in after school and made sense of it. I started entering the new puppies' information into the computer on the counter, making up cute names in my head for each new pup that I entered. The German shepherd puppy I nicknamed Hans, and the toy poodle was Heidi. I smiled to myself and the work flew by.

By the time I'd finished entering the data, Lori had brought Eric back. He looked overwhelmed, but he nodded when she asked him if he'd like to feed the dogs.

"I'll show him," I told Lori. "I did the file updates."

"Already?" Lori turned to Eric. "This girl's a wonder." Then she turned back to me and winked.

I felt my face turning pink so I grabbed the sleeve of Eric's T-shirt and started dragging him into the kennel area.

"Okay, we'll just do the feeding now," I called over my shoulder.

"Lori seems really nice," Eric said, a smile playing around his lips.

"Yeah, she's a wonder," I said drily, and he laughed. "So, each dog's portion size is based on their weight—which is listed here on the chart." I stopped at the first crate and reached through the bars to pet the big gray mutt on the head. He licked my hand and sat up, starting his excitement dance because he knew food was coming. "Don't reach through the bars of all of them," I told Eric. "Most of them are okay, but I don't know about the new guys yet. Probably better let me check them out first and I'll tell you if you can pet."

"How long's this guy been here?" Eric asked me.

I frowned. "This is Rufus—and a long time, at least two months. I'm really hoping we can find a good home for him." I reached through and patted his head again. "You're a good boy, aren't you, Rufus?"

"Poor guy," Eric said, sounding like he meant it. "I wish there was more I could do. Besides feeding him, I mean."

"Well, you could volunteer the next time we have an adoption fair downtown," I told him. "You could use some of that presidential charm of yours to convince some nice family to adopt Rufus."

"*Presidential charm?*" Eric repeated, and I turned pink—and then red. I guessed that was a term I had only used in my head . . . until just now.

"You know what I mean," I said, trying hard not to make a run for it.

Eric smirked. "I really don't. Maybe you could give me an *example* of my charm," he went on.

I glared at him. "I can give you an example of your *lack* of charm right now, but that's the best I can do. Come on, let me show you how to measure the food."

Then I kept up a steady stream of instructions so that Eric couldn't make any further comments about me noticing his charm.

Arghh

1. Math homework

2. Potato-less days

3. Too-many-baked-potato days (at Aunt Pam's house)

4. Accidentally pointing out Eric Chung's charm

16

Penultimate means "next to last"

"Lovely to see you, too, Mrs. Carlson, Mrs. Levi," Eric was saying to a pair of older ladies. The crowd at the Winsted Winner's Circle was definitely an older one. Eric had introduced me to at least seven of somebody's grandparents already.

"See, this is what I meant," I hissed in his ear as the two ladies moved off.

"What you meant when?" Eric asked.

I shifted Potato from one arm to the other. "The other day when I said you were presidential. I meant that you were good with grown-ups. That's what I mean about what I . . . meant," I finished, and sighed, realizing how badly the sentence had gotten away from me.

Eric raised his eyebrows. "You said I was presidentially *charming*, actually," he corrected, with a half smile, and I glared at him. Why had I brought up that embarrassing comment again? I put Potato down and started to root around the bag Mrs. Chung had packed for us, looking for the doggy brush.

"I think I should brush him one more time," I told Eric.

"Sure. We want him to look his best so he can *charm* the judges."

"Ughh!" I found the brush, and I threw the rest of the bag at his chest while he laughed.

"I've been checking out the competition," Lily said, running up to us in a rush. "I think you've got it in the bag. Potato's by far the cutest."

"They don't judge on cuteness," Eric told her.

Lily frowned. "I know. And that's really disappointing. Maybe we could enter him in a doggy beauty pageant instead?"

"You find one of those, we'll enter him," her brother said.

I finished brushing Potato and picked him back up. The three of us made our way over to the center of the action. Mrs. Chung had come with us to sign in, since none of us were officially old enough to enter a dog in the show, but then she'd left us to go get her nails done. She was supportive, obviously, but she clearly didn't seem to care too much about this small dog show. Not to mention the fact that Potato was the rescue pup Eric was trying to turn into a show dog to prove a point to her.

The show was being held in the town square, just a few blocks from Orphan Paws. There was an area set up for the dogs to promenade, and a small table of judges. Only a handful of spectators—including Lily—sat on the benches and chairs scattered across the grass. It didn't look much like the only other dog show I'd ever seen, which was on TV, and was much bigger and fancier. In that show, the trainers and owners all wore nice dresses and suits. Here, most people were fairly casual, in pants or skirts. I was glad I hadn't thrown on my usual uniform of jeans and a hoodie. I wore black pants I'd dug out of my cousin's closet and a light blue cardigan. I had to admit Eric looked annoyingly handsome in a blue polo shirt and gray slacks.

"So you remember what to do?" Eric was asking me as a voice on a megaphone called out for all small-breeds to assemble. I put Potato down beside me.

"I think so. I mean, it's not that complicated," I replied, even though I did feel a rush of nervousness.

"I was just checking." Eric pulled something sparkly out of his pocket and bent down to Potato's level.

"What's *that*?"

"His new collar."

"Why is it . . . bedazzled?"

"They're just rhinestones. I'm personally not a huge fan of it myself, but I heard through the dog-show grapevine that sparkly collars give you a leg up. Potato needs to put his best foot forward."

"Uh, I think you mean *paw*," Lily pointed out, and Eric groaned. Meanwhile, I was still chuckling over the term *dog-show grapevine*.

"I guess, welcome to show business," I told Potato. "You can take that off when this is over," I promised him. I'd swear from his expression he was not happy about his new bling.

"Okay, this is it." Eric led the way to where the trainers were lining up with their dogs.

"When they call your name, just lead him around the circle. Then take him to that table over there and the judges will check him out."

"Okay." I nodded, my stomach tightening. Why should I be nervous? Why did I care?

I watched as a lady in a maxiskirt led her Havanese around the circle—the dog trotted perfectly, all around, and then a man with the German pinscher took their place. None of the dogs seemed to have any trouble until a long-haired dachshund kept stopping every few paces and looking expectantly up at his owner or trainer. She pulled him along after each stop, clearly embarrassed. Finally, it was our turn.

I led Potato out, and he followed me. I was holding my breath as he started trotting—he was doing perfectly. We were halfway around—and everything was going well.

Until a dog treat fell out of my pocket.

Potato stopped in his tracks and went back to retrieve it.

I looked up in shock at Eric, who was motioning for me to keep going, so I pulled Potato's new black leash gently and he finished the circle with me.

I was trembling a little as I brought Potato over to the judges' table. Eric joined me while the judges measured and patted Potato.

"Where did that treat come from?" Eric whispered.

"It fell out of my pocket," I explained with a sigh. "I'm really sorry!"

And I was. As much as I thought the whole dog show competition was kind of dumb, some part of me had wanted Potato to do well. I hated that I'd been the one to mess it up.

After a beat Eric said, "It's okay. We'll just have to remember to unload your pockets next time."

"You mean you'd let me lead him around again?" I asked, surprised. We were interrupted then by the judges giving Potato back to us. Eric took him this time, and rubbed his head and told him he'd done a good job.

I couldn't help but smile.

"Sure," Eric said. "Rookie mistake—it could happen to anyone. You should have seen my first show."

"He won first place," Lily broke in, joining us again. "So if he's trying to be modest, he's lying."

I couldn't figure out if I wanted to glare at Eric or thank him for trying to make me feel better.

"Do you guys want to go to Max's for some ice cream while we wait for the results?" Lily asked.

"I think we know what the results will be," I said gloomily.

Lily linked her arm through mine. "Cheer up, little camper. Some chocolate with sprinkles will make everything better."

"Make it butter pecan in a sugar cone, and you might just be right," I said.

As the judges whispered at the table, Eric, Lily, and I crossed the street to Max's. We got our cones to go—Eric agreed to let Potato have a small cup of vanilla to celebrate him finishing his first show. Then we sat on a bench in the town square, trying not to watch the judges as they deliberated.

"What about the rally part?" I asked Eric as I licked my butter pecan. "I thought you were going to have him do the obstacle course thing?"

Eric shook his head, wiping a spot of mint chocolate chip from the corner of his mouth. "I think we should save that for next time. It takes a lot of stamina, and it wouldn't be a bad idea for him to keep getting stronger for a while."

"Okay," I said. I was touched that he seemed to really have Potato's health in mind. "I really am sorry about the dog cookie. I don't even know how it fell out." I pulled my pocket inside out . . . and that's when I noticed the hole. "Oh, man—yeah, I do!" I put my finger through the hole in the pocket and waggled it to show them. I guess that's what I got for wearing my cousin's ancient pants.

"Well, that's one mystery solved," Lily said.

We heard the town's loudspeaker crackle. The head judge told us that the winners were about to be announced. I felt my stomach jump as I gathered up Potato and we hurried over to the judges' table. We were just in time to hear that the German pinscher had won, followed by the Havanese. The rest of the rankings were written on a large whiteboard propped in front of the makeshift stage.

I rushed over to read the results. It didn't take long to find Potato's name—since this show wasn't formal, we could stick with Potato as his show name. He was listed next to last—just above Peanut, the distracted dachshund.

"Next to last," Eric said. "Well, at least it's not last."

I picked up Potato and gave him a kiss. "Good job, buddy—even with my defective pocket hole, you came in penultimate!"

"Pen-what?" Lily asked.

"*Penultimate* means 'next to last,'" Eric said.

I grinned at him. "Yeah, but it sure does sound better, doesn't it?"

17

Unexpected invite

"If it weren't for the pocket hole, he would've done really well," Eric was telling Lori the next day, filling her in on Potato's show business debut.

Lori frowned sympathetically. "You shouldn't make Cecilia feel bad about the pocket," she told him. "She lost most of her clothes in the fire a few weeks ago, remember?"

Eric turned to me in surprise, holding the crate liner he'd been about to rinse off. "What fire?"

I glared at Lori. "Well, my house sort of burned down," I said, not meeting his eyes. "I mean, not down as in *to the ground*, but it got condemned after the fire, so . . ." I trailed off, feeling embarrassed at having to tell this story to Eric. The Chungs' house—wiring and all—was super new.

"I didn't know," he said quietly. I realized Lori was heading back out front after dropping the bomb about my house. I could hear the click-clack of her sparkly shoes as she made her escape. "I just figured you always lived with your aunt. I'm really sorry."

"Not your fault," I mumbled, untangling the hose from around my feet and drying off the plastic liner he handed me.

"I didn't mean . . . hey, if you don't want to talk about it, it's cool."

"Thanks," I said. I *didn't* feel like talking about it.

"So, what're you up to next weekend?" he asked me, and I looked up quickly in surprise.

"Is there another dog show?" I asked.

Eric smiled and shook his head. "No." He looked away from me and hosed off another crate liner. "I was just, um, wondering if you wanted to go with me—and Lily—to the Spring Bash?"

The Spring Bash? The school dance had barely registered on my radar, because I'd never planned to go. "I thought Lily was going with Joey Lewis?" was the only thing I could come up with as a response. I knew Lily had had a crush on Joey forever, and she was super excited when he'd texted her last week to ask her to the dance.

Eric still wasn't looking at me as he reached for the next dirty crate liner from the pile. "She is—I just meant that the four of us could go. You would get to hang out with Lily . . . and you and I could go as friends. What do you say?"

As friends. I tried not to let those words sink in, or wonder why they bothered me.

"I'm still trying to figure out what *you* said," I told him. Eric seemed to let out a breath he'd been holding. "I've never been to one of those things," I admitted, blushing. I thought of what Mel would say, and Lori, and Dad. About me coming out of my turtle shell some more. And it had been kind of nice, being out of that shell—spending time with Lily, and even Eric. "I guess it might be fun," I said at last.

"We can celebrate Potato's first show," he added.

"Okay, sure," I said. He smiled and went back to the hose, cool as a cucumber.

I watched him, feeling totally confused. Did Lily know he'd asked me to go to the dance? Had she put him up to it? He'd gone to almost ridiculous lengths to make it clear he was asking me *just as a friend*. Which was fine, I thought. After all, a few weeks ago, I'd hated the guy. But now . . .

When I got home from O.P., I climbed the stairs to my borrowed room. I took the little cup from the bathroom and watered my cactus, as I did every week or so.

Whatever the circumstances, I, Cecilia Murray, was going to a school dance! I opened my closet. Too bad my cousin hadn't left behind any fancy dresses. I'd have to talk my aunt into taking me shopping. I hoped I could survive the ordeal.

I sat in front of the computer to try to Skype Mel, but she wasn't online.

She was probably out doing something social. And come Saturday, I would be, too.

A surprising to-do list

1. Buy a dress

2. Get a haircut (ask Aunt Pam to take me)

3. Figure out how to do makeup (ask Mel and/or Lily for help)

4. Find accessories (can't let Potato be the only one with bling)

18

Pumpkin time

"No, just smile in a *normal* way," my dad was saying as he held up his phone to take a picture of me and Eric before the dance. We were standing outside Aunt Pam's house. Thankfully, she was out with friends; I didn't need her witnessing this humiliation.

I responded by crossing my eyes and sticking out my tongue at him.

"Well, *that's* much better," Dad said.

Eric seemed nervous for some reason. He kept checking his watch like we were late to catch a bus or something. I thought maybe he was worried that Dad was going to sit him down for some kind of manly talk before we got out of there.

"He does realize we're just going as friends, right?" Eric asked me as my father continued to document the event. Suspicion confirmed.

"I told him," I sighed. I got it. We were *just* friends. Why was he making such a big deal out of it?

"Put your arm around her! She won't bite," Dad called.

"I might bite *you*," I snapped. Dad's face fell, and then I felt immediately guilty. "It's just, we're going to be late for the dance," I explained. Meanwhile, I was relieved that Eric *hadn't* put his arm around me, as instructed.

"I guess I've got enough." Dad almost smiled at me. "I'll bring the car around—you two wait here."

"I can't wait until we're old enough to drive ourselves," Eric said as Dad went off to get the car.

"Me neither. Look, I'm sorry about my dad . . ."

He made a waving motion with one hand. "Nah. He's fine. My dad can be much more embarrassing, I promise. One time, he brought all of our dogs to my first big school event as student council president. It would have been fun, if Sulu hadn't barfed all over the principal's shoes," he said with a laugh. We started walking down my aunt's driveway toward the curb. "Hey, so why are you walking like that?"

I sighed loudly. "Well, I've never actually walked in heels before . . ."

Two days ago, Aunt Pam had taken me shopping, and she'd been in heaven. At first, I'd been miserable as we wandered around the mall but then slowly but surely, I started to actually—maybe, sort of—enjoy myself.

Especially when I'd found a beautiful dress and went to try it on. It was black and sleeveless, with a black ribbon that tied around the waist, and a pleated bottom that swirled just a little when I twirled around in front of the mirror. But the best part was that the top part had a dusting of tiny sparkles that caught the light.

"You're too young to wear black," Aunt Pam had argued. "You should wear *color*."

"I like black," I told her.

"She looks good in it! And black is very in right now." That was FaceTime Mel on my aunt's phone. I gave my best friend a grateful smile. Aunt Pam finally listened when it was *Mel's* fashion opinion. My aunt always said Mel's clothing was "very becoming for a young woman."

So we got the dress, and then I even let Aunt Pam drag me to get new shoes—the strappy black sandals I now wobbled in. The heels weren't even *that* high, but when all you wear are Converse sneakers and flats, any sort of heel is kind of a problem.

Still, I couldn't help enjoying the feeling of being dressed up. Earlier today, Aunt Pam had taken me to get my hair cut. When I got home, I changed into my new dress and the shoes, and then stood in front of the mirror that hung on the back of the bathroom door. Now that my hair was shorter, it wasn't quite so flat. I'd very carefully added a little bit of the brown eyeliner Skype Mel had shown me how to use. Then I put on some tinted lip balm and stepped back.

The mirror was a little old and cloudy, but as I studied my reflection I could swear I looked kind of . . . pretty.

Then, when Eric had rung the bell at my aunt's house, looking handsome as ever in a navy-blue suit, his jaw had dropped when he'd seen me.

"Hey . . . um, Cecilia . . . ?" Eric—Mr. President himself!—had been speechless.

"It's me." I laughed, though Eric had still looked dazed. Which may have been worth the whole shopping expedition with Aunt Pam.

Now Eric was still looking at me like he barely recognized me as we got into Dad's car. Lily was riding to the dance with Joey Lewis, so she'd meet us there.

Dad dropped us off, and we walked across the wide entrance to the school, me concentrating very carefully on not falling in my new shoes.

Lily came running up to us as soon as we walked in. She was wearing a pink dress. I wouldn't normally say I was a fan of pink dresses, but hers was really cute and matched her personality. It was cheerful and had a wide sash of darker pink. She wore little pink flats to match.

"C—you look amazing!" She hugged me, then pulled back to examine the dress. "This dress! And I love your shoes."

"Thanks." I shifted from one foot to the other. "I may need to hang on to you for support." I looked around. "Where's Joey?"

Lily shrugged. "Unknown. He doesn't dance anyway, so he's really more of a photo prop. You wanna come dance?"

"Where did Eric go?"

Lily pointed. "Over there with the basketball boys, where else? Come on." She dragged me by the hand and pulled me with her into a circle of her other friends—Allie Cross and a few of the pep squad members. They all smiled at me when we joined their group. I felt awkward at first, trying not to look silly in front of these popular girls, but then we all started talking about how hard Mr. Key's last test was, and I stopped feeling uncomfortable at all.

Allie and a few of the others said they liked the next song and went to go dance. Lily turned to me and said, "Punch?" I nodded, following her off the floor.

We walked over to one of the little tables and I saw Eric was sitting there, talking to a very pretty girl I'd never seen before. I felt a stab of something that felt like jealousy.

Eric stood up when we approached. "Hi," he said. He seemed sort of awkward all of a sudden. "This is Destiny," he said to me and Lily. "She goes to Northridge—she's here with Austin."

"Hi," Lily and I said in unison to Destiny, who was very tiny and had extremely shiny blond hair.

"So, Eric," Lily said, "since I can't find Joey, how about you go get some punch for me and your *date*?" As she said the word *date*, she gave Destiny the side eye. Lily knew Eric and I were going as friends, but I appreciated her protectiveness of me all the same.

"I love punch," I added, then winced as I realized how dumb that must have sounded.

Eric looked confused but he didn't say anything else before going off to get us some of that punch I loved so much.

Lily and I sat down. "So you go to Northridge," Lily said to Destiny.

"Yes. It's in Winchester."

"Yep." I nodded. "It sure is."

Several seconds passed in awkward silence.

Lily stood up abruptly and pulled me along with her. "We're going to the bathroom," she told the other girl.

"Okay. Bye."

"She's quite the conversationalist," I said to Lily as she dragged me with her away from the table.

"I was just going to say the same thing about you! I mean, using a smaller word, but still. What's up with you? Do you know you're being weird?" It was clear Lily's bathroom trip was just an excuse to confront me away from Destiny.

I considered her words for a second, then nodded. "I really think I am."

Lily let out an exasperated breath. "Well, do you know *why* you're being so weird?" I knew she was trying to get at something, and I *thought* I knew what it was, but I chose to stay quiet.

I shook my head.

Eric appeared then, carefully carrying four cups of punch. Lily and I made our way back to the table.

Eric handed the fourth cup to Destiny, who accepted it with a flirtatious smile. *Ugh.* Lily was looking from me to Eric. We all sat down and drank our punch. Lily made another attempt to talk to Destiny. "So what kinds of activities do you do at your school?"

"I'm on the dance team," she said, but then didn't offer any more information.

"Great." Lily nodded, then started looking around the gym—possibly for Austin Fuller, Destiny's missing date.

Eric wasn't holding up his end of the conversation at all, which was very unusual for him. He spent most of his time looking down at his punch or making the occasional joke about the DJ's song choices. Was he nervous around Destiny? Or maybe he'd been blinded by her shiny hair.

Why does this all feel so weird? I'm just here with Eric as a friend. Why should I care how he acts around Destiny?

After what seemed like a long time with the four of us sitting there in mostly awkward silence, Austin and Joey came over. Lily stood up and took Joey's arm, and I was relieved when Destiny flitted off with Austin.

The tension between Eric and me eased, but then came back with a vengeance: A slow song had started.

Eric stood up, too, and moved around to my side of the table. I'd been sitting with Lily on one side and Destiny on the other.

"Do you want to dance?" he asked.

I felt a stab of nervous fear go through my stomach. I'd never danced with a boy before. I'd seen slow dances in a million movies and TV shows, but this was different—this was real life.

Mutely, I nodded, stood up, and then tripped and started to fall forward. Eric reached out fast and caught me.

How embarrassing! "The heels," I reminded him. Then a moment of inspiration hit. I held on to his arm as I took off both shoes. I bent and picked them up with one hand. I realized then that I was still holding on to his arm with my other hand.

"Better?" Eric asked me.

"Much." I smiled up at him, back to my normal height. And, hopefully, back to being able to walk.

I put the shoes on the chair I'd been sitting in and followed Eric out to the dance floor. Very slowly, he put his arm around my waist. My heart jumped at the sensation, but I tried not to blush. We both moved to the music. It was a song I'd never heard, but I liked it right away.

The song sped up a bit. Eric pulled me just a little bit closer to him. I looked up at him, swallowing hard.

"Thanks for bringing me to this," I told him, searching my brain for something clever to say.

"You're welcome. I thought you could use a night off from saving the world's dogs."

I studied his face. A lot of times when people said stuff like that, they were making fun of me. But it didn't seem like he was. I hoped he wasn't.

"I should thank you for coming with *me*," Eric added. "After all, I know this stuff isn't really your thing."

"No, I like dancing. And it turns out I don't mind dressing up either. Just maybe not in heels . . ." I realized that I was rambling, so I trailed off, looking down at my bare feet.

"For someone so quiet, you always have a lot to say," Eric said in an amused voice. He lowered his head so that it was close to mine.

I stared at him. "I know," I said. "Sorry. But if it makes you feel any better, eventually I talk too much with everyone."

"And here I thought I was special."

You are, said the voice in my head, and I'm sure the surprise I felt showed on my face. I tried to think of something safe to say out loud, but I couldn't think of anything. The song ended then, and we stepped apart.

"Thank you for the dance," I told him. I felt butterflies in my stomach, then mentally tried to shoo them away. *We're just friends*, I repeated to myself. But with that dance, I couldn't help but wonder if there was maybe something more.

"No problem." He grinned and led me back to the table, where I sat back down beside Lily. Her friend Emily from pep squad was already talking to her about some girl who used to go to school with us, someone I didn't know. I told Lily I'd be right back and put on my shoes, wobbling painfully toward the bathroom.

When I left the restroom, I started to turn the corner back toward the gym when I heard my name.

"Eric, man, I just gotta ask. *What* are you doing with Cecilia Murray?" It was Austin Fuller's voice. I froze in my tracks.

"She's that weird girl in our history class," I heard another voice say.

I heard Eric laugh and say, "She's just a friend of my sister's."

My heart pounded. A small part of me hoped that Eric and I had made some sort of connection tonight, a bond deeper than just puppy co-trainers. Certainly a bond deep enough for him to defend me against less-than-nice comments.

Eric was saying more, but I needed to get out of there and clear my head. I kicked off my shoes in anger, leaving the dreaded things behind. I quickly grabbed my backup sneakers from my locker and used the phone behind the desk in the library to call my aunt's house. My dad didn't understand why he had to pick me up at the back of the school. And when I got into the car, he also wondered where my shoes were, but when I didn't answer, he didn't push.

I ran upstairs as soon as we got home. I knew Lily would wonder what had happened to me, and I wished I had a phone to text her. I'd just have to explain it to her on Monday.

The problem was, I didn't even know how to explain. Why had Eric's words hurt so much? Eric had told me straight out that he was only asking me to the dance as a friend. He hadn't really done or said anything so horrible. Or had he? He'd flirted with that Destiny girl. He'd called me a friend of his *sister's*—not even his friend. And he'd laughed at me along with his friends, not even bothering to defend me when they called me weird.

I curled into a ball on top of the quilt on my borrowed bed, still in my pretty new dress. There in the dark I was finally able to admit the truth. The whole night had made me feel just a little bit like Cinderella. After all, I'd busted out of my usual life of cleaning up after the puppies at O.P. Wearing the new dress and makeup, and especially dancing with Eric, had been almost exactly like a fairy tale.

But my Cinderella moment was over. I knew that my carriage had just turned back into a pumpkin.

I'd thought maybe I was changing. But I guessed I was still the weird turtle girl after all.

I'd also begun to think that maybe I'd been wrong about Eric. But now I realized that I'd been right at first when I decided that he was an arrogant jerk.

19
Nothing like Cinderella

It was the shoes that gave me away.

I walked to Orphan Paws on Monday morning; we had the day off from school because of a teacher meeting.

Lori took one look at my melancholy face and knew not to ask me how the dance went. She simply gave me a huge hug and told me I could go home if I wanted to. But the last thing I wanted to do was sit alone in my tiny room replaying the scene at the end of the dance. So I asked for a job and she gave me one: inventorying the medical supplies in the back closet.

Once I removed everything from the shelves, I let myself get lost in counting the boxes of gauze and bandages and antiseptics. The shelves were pretty dusty, and I was sneezing a lot. I went into the restroom and grabbed a handful of toilet paper to stuff in my pocket for when my nose started running.

I don't know how much time passed before Lori came back and said, "Cecilia, you have a visitor."

I rounded the corner into the intake room of the shelter and there was Eric Chung.

Lori stood there smiling, but there was a tightness behind it, as if she knew Eric might have been the cause of my bad mood. "Your helper's back!" she announced in a failed attempt to make things not awkward. "Let me know if you need me," she whispered to me, then quickly left the room.

Eric was holding up my strappy black shoes. "Lose something?"

I tried to snatch them away from him, but he held them up higher than my reach for some reason. Still looking at me, in all my toilet-paper-in-pocket glory, he said in a quieter voice, "I was right, then. You heard."

"Of course I heard. You know I was there. You're holding my shoes."

"I was bringing them back to you," he said. "But mostly I came to apologize."

"Okay." I turned away and started throwing the toilet paper into the nearest trash can. "There's nothing to be sorry about. But thank you for bringing them, I guess."

"How did you get all the way home without your shoes?"

I felt a surge of anger. "What do *you* care how I got home? I'm just your sister's weird friend, remember?"

"Cecilia, I'm really sorry." He took a step forward, but then stopped, looking like he didn't know what to do. Which was strange since Eric Chung never looked like that, except for the one time he'd asked me for help with Potato. "I—I didn't think you'd be there listening. I didn't mean to hurt your feelings. It's just . . . it's sometimes hard to explain to my friends about my dog show life. They tease me a lot, and I—I just didn't want to explain how we know each other, and that I am training yet another dog. *Another dog?* they'd say."

My mind flashed to the several times that Mel and my dad had all said the exact same thing to me.

"And the *weird* comment . . . the guys were just joking around so I went along with it. I didn't mean . . . it's just, actually, I *like* that you can be weird, Cecilia. You're . . . different from any other girl. You're really . . . cool."

He was staring into my eyes, which was making it hard to pretend that I was fine. I couldn't tell if he was being honest or if he was just trying to guarantee that he still had someone to help him with Potato.

But then I heard his voice on repeat in my head saying, *She's just a friend of my sister's.* Here I'd been thinking maybe we could be more than friends—and Eric didn't even think of me as *his* friend.

"You didn't hurt my feelings," I lied. "I'm one hundred percent fine. So you can leave the shoes and go. Since Lily and I are friends, we'll probably have to see each other again. But we don't have to be friends. We'll be . . ." I trailed off, thinking of the right word.

"Civil?" He sort of smiled when he said it, but it was a strange smile. Not a happy one.

It took me a few seconds to respond. "Yeah. Civil. Fantastic. That. Let's be civil." I turned to go back to my inventory closet, but he put a hand on my arm to stop me.

"Cecilia, wait."

I turned back around. I realized he still had the shoes so I held out a hand for them without looking at him. I was too embarrassed at this point to make eye contact. When the shoes didn't show up, I raised my head in confusion.

He exhaled loudly. "I was really hoping you could forgive me for being such a jerk. Maybe someday you will. I'm not going to stop trying to get you to. Because . . . I . . . we . . . Potato and I still really need your help."

Potato. I was tempted to back out of our deal, but the image of my dad lying on the couch, depressed, flickered into my head, reminding me of why I had agreed to help Eric in the first place. I also couldn't bear the thought of losing my Potato forever.

"I know. You do need my help," I said coolly. Then another question occurred to me, a question I hadn't asked because I was worried he'd get mad. But now that *we* weren't friends, what was stopping me?

"Why do you care about this so much?" I demanded. "Honestly. Why does Potato have to be paraded around a bunch of snobs, and measured, and poked, and prodded? Why can't you just love him? If I could have kept him . . ." My voice caught, and I stopped talking.

Eric frowned, looking down. He took a deep breath and let it out. He looked conflicted. "The very first dog we ever adopted was a rescue dog. His name was Porkchop, and I loved him. But then my parents started getting into the dog-show business, and all of a sudden we had a bunch of fancy, expensive dogs in the family, too." He paused and ran a hand through his dark hair. "We love all of the dogs we have, but a part of me always felt that my parents loved Porkchop less because he never competed. And, well, Porkchop died a few months ago, and my parents didn't even seem that sad about it. So when I adopted Potato, I wanted to prove to my parents that rescue dogs are worthy of love, too. And I know that the only way to do it is to have him win a dog show. For me. And for Porkchop."

I stared at Eric, unsure of what to say. He had laid everything on the table, and I knew he was telling the truth. But I couldn't quite reconcile the two Erics that stood before me: the jerk who'd mocked me with his friends, and this sweet dog lover who wanted to make an important point.

I definitely didn't want to prove to his parents that rescue dogs were somehow *less than* purebreds. Plus, there was still a cash prize on the line, and I wasn't ready to let that go. I, too, had a point I needed to make. A point to my dad, that I could help him and help our family.

"I'm also concerned," Eric continued, "that if Potato *isn't* dog show material, they'll make me give him up. They let me adopt him under the condition that I take full responsibility for him. They were really hesitant about it, though, so I worry that if Potato doesn't earn his keep in the dog-show circuit, he might no longer have a space in the Chung household. I know this would be important to you since you want him to have a home, but it'd be good for me, too—I'm growing pretty attached to the little guy."

My heart broke a little at the thought of Potato having to move out of his comfy surroundings. Of course I'd want Potato to keep his home, even if it was with Eric.

"So . . . is our deal still on?" Eric seemed uncomfortable with my silence. I realized then that I had not yet confirmed or denied whether I was backing out.

I closed my eyes, cringing. Helping Eric was the last thing I wanted to do, but I had too many other reasons to keep going.

"Our deal is still on," I confirmed, opening my eyes.

He looked relieved. "Okay. I'll see you tomorrow after school?"

I nodded. "Yes. Now please go away."

Eric gave me one last look, one I couldn't figure out, before he did what I asked.

Lori popped back in seconds later, taking in my distraught expression.

"What's wrong?" she asked, coming over. "I knew I shouldn't have let him in. Do I need to knock some sense into that boy?"

Lori balled up her fists, which were decorated with several pretty rings, and started boxing at the air.

I couldn't help but giggle at the sight. "No, it's fine, Lori." I thought for a moment. "Have you ever had to do something you didn't want to do but did it anyway because you knew you had to?" I knew I wasn't being super clear, but I was hoping Lori understood me all the same.

"All the time, kid, all the time." Lori dropped her fists and looked at me sympathetically. "Listen, I don't know what's going on with you, and I don't want you to tell me if you're not comfortable. But I want you to know that you're awesome. And whoever can't see that doesn't deserve you in their life."

I nodded, blushing a little. "Thanks, Lori."

"It's really too bad about that boy, though," Lori added. "At first I thought it was really sweet—him bringing you the shoes you left at the dance. Sort of like Cinderella."

I shook my head at her, then rolled my eyes for emphasis. "He was not being Prince Charming, I promise you."

Lori gave a short laugh, then darted out of the room. From the delighted barks I heard from the front, I was guessing the dogs were happy to see Lori again. She was the kind of person who made every place she went just a little brighter.

I turned back to finish up the inventory, but my mind kept wandering. As heartfelt as the Porkchop story was, could Eric just be using me to turn Potato into a superstar? Would he and I ever be real friends?

And why did I care so darn much?

Reasons to help train Potato

1. Potato time

2. Money for Dad

3. ~~Eric is not as bad as I thought~~

20

Team Murray

"So it's called the what now?" I asked Eric.

"The Southern Connecticut Association Rally . . ."

"It's called SCAR? Seriously?"

"You didn't let me finish . . . it's the Southern Connecticut Association Rally *and* Dog Show. So that would be SCARDS, which isn't a thing. Besides, they don't use the letters anyway."

"So Potato is signed up for this whole thing already?" I asked doubtfully. "It sounds like a big deal."

"He's going to compete in the show portion. I told you, I decided that Potato won't be competing in the rally part again this time." Eric was using his patient voice, which made me want to strangle him even more. Even several days after the dance, I could still feel tension between us. My defenses were way up. I tuned back in to what Eric was saying. "Potato needs to build up some more muscle tone."

I sighed and looked back into Lily's bedroom, where she sat cross-legged on her floor. I'd come over after school to do homework with her and also see Potato. Now being cornered by Mr. Dog Show was super annoying.

"I was thinking we could get back to training," Eric continued.

"Sure," I said, swallowing all the mean thoughts that came through my head. I knew I had agreed to help, but I was still resentful of everything that had happened between Eric and me. "Whenever you're ready."

"Okay," Eric said carefully, looking like he didn't want to press his luck.

When he was gone, I walked back into Lily's room and threw myself down onto the spare bed. "What happened between you two?" Lily asked, looking up from the book she was reading.

"What do you mean?" I sat up and pretended that finding my pencil was a very difficult job that took all my attention.

"I thought you guys were getting to be friends, maybe. Eric would even joke around with you. He doesn't do that with everybody. But then since the dance, he's back to being all awkward with you. And you seem mad at him. Did he do something?"

I'd come up with the magical excuse of a stomach virus to explain my quick getaway from the Spring Bash, which apparently, Lily had bought. Now I just had to get her off the trail of figuring out why I was mad at her brother.

"No, he didn't do anything."

"Are you sure? Because if you want me to talk to him . . ."

"No! I mean, you don't need to! I'm fine. He's fine. Everyone's fine." The rush of words that came out clearly startled Lily.

She stared. "Yeah, because you sound really *super* fine right now. What's *wrong*?"

I threw myself back against the bed again. As much as I wanted to confide in Lily, the fact was, I couldn't. She was Eric's twin sister. I didn't want to put her in the middle like that. I had a feeling she might even be really mad at her brother if I told her the whole story, and I didn't want to cause a fight. "Nothing. I'm just being dramatic," I told her.

"Okay. I guess tell me when you're ready." Lily slammed her textbook shut. "Do you want to watch a movie?" she asked me.

I nodded and pushed thoughts of Eric way into the back of my mind. For the moment, I tried to simply enjoy snuggling with Potato in front of Lily's TV.

On Wednesday morning, at my locker, Lily asked me to stay over on the weekend again.

"There's a *carnival* coming to the mall in Winchester!" she announced.

"A carnival?"

"It's just one of those little traveling ones. I saw the signs for it when I was shopping with my mom the other day. We *have* to go—I'm dying for some cotton candy."

I laughed at how excited Lily seemed to be about cotton candy. "Do they have rides?"

"Of course! And, as mentioned before, cotton candy."

I hesitated, thinking about what it would be like to spend that much time with Eric. But the notion of getting to see Potato, and hang out with Lily, was too compelling. I could just ignore Eric.

"Just ignore him," Mel had advised when we'd Skyped yesterday. I'd filled her in on the whole drama at the dance, and Mel had been sympathetic. Then she'd also cheered me up with some good news: She'd be coming back to visit soon! She had spring break and had convinced her parents that they needed to spend time back in their old hometown.

Now the thought of Mel getting to meet Lily—and Potato—brightened my spirits enough to answer Lily in an upbeat way.

"I'm in," I said. "As long as I can get a ride over there? My dad's got a case and he's been working all the time." Despite the extra hours he'd been putting in lately, my dad seemed to be in better spirits, so I was hoping his job was stressing him out less.

"Sure," Lily said. "My mom or dad can drive you. They both think you're great, you know! They're always saying how you're so much more polite than any of my other friends."

Great, I thought wryly. So all the members of the Chung family liked me. Except, of course, Eric.

The next night, I was putting clothes into my old backpack as Dad sat on the edge of the bed pretending to decide whether or not to let me stay over at the Chungs' again this weekend. I pretty much knew he'd let me, since it was a social thing, and he'd been trying to get me to do social things forever. But since I was over there a lot, he seemed to think the code of parenting included a rule that he had to protest spending so much time apart from his beloved child.

"Are you sure they don't mind you being over there so often?" Dad was asking, for the second time.

"*They* invited *me*," I told him (also a rerun).

Dad sighed and paused for a second. "I'm sorry we're stuck here at Aunt Pam's, C."

I dropped the jeans I'd been folding. "What?"

"I'm sorry we have to stay here and mooch off your aunt. It wasn't my plan."

I sat down beside him. "It's fine—where's this coming from?"

Dad gave me a sad look. "I *heard* you. The night we went to Chili's. Talking to Mel on Skype."

I felt a wave of shame wash over me, and my face felt hot. What could I say? I *had* complained about getting stuck with Aunt Pamela. But I didn't mean for him to hear that. I was just getting stuff off my chest. *This must mean he also heard what I said about him not having enough money*, I thought grimly.

"I'm sorry," I said. "I really am. It just . . . it was really hard losing our house. I didn't mean to make you feel bad."

To my shock, Dad looked like he had tears in his eyes. "I'm not telling you this because I'm mad at you. I really am sorry we lost the house, too, and that this was the best I could do right now. Like I said, none of this was in the plan."

I looked at him for a few seconds. Dad had been so grumpy and sit-aroundy for so long, I had to admit it was a little surprising to hear him talk this way.

"The house wasn't anybody's fault," I said softly. "But . . . Dad, can I ask, what *was* your plan?"

He leaned back against the wall. "The plan was for me to make a go of it as a lawyer. *Not* to make less money than I did as a teacher. I want to provide a good home for you, and I feel terrible that I haven't been able to do that. I'm sorry we've had to stay at your aunt's for so long."

"Oh." This was a lot of information to take in.

"Yeah. I'm sorry—I didn't mean to lay all this heavy stuff on you. Money shouldn't be your worry."

"You can tell me what's going on. I'm not a baby anymore," I reminded him.

Dad chuckled. "Cecilia, you haven't been a baby for a long time."

"Dad? Do you *like* being a lawyer?"

He looked surprised. "Yes, I do. I really do, actually. It's just—I guess I had this idea of what it would be like. I love helping out people who really need it, but money's a lot tighter than I thought it'd be."

"But this new case . . . it seems like it's going well?"

Dad smiled. "I don't want to jinx it, but . . . I think it is."

"That's great, Dad. The liking-your-job part, I mean. You know I'm rooting for you. You worked really hard to get here. I think you're a great lawyer. The money stuff is less important."

And just then, it occurred to me that I maybe didn't need dog-show prize money to show my dad how much I supported him. I could just let him know myself.

"I also don't think you've done a bad job finding a home for us," I added, choking up a little. "I'm fine wherever we live as long as I have you. We're a team, Dad."

Dad hugged me then, for the first time since the fire, and for the first time in forever when he *wasn't* just hugging me because I'd just survived a fire. I hugged him back, and it was the best feeling in the world.

Dad stood up, brushing tears from his eyes, and smiled down at me. Then he rubbed his back. "Well, I don't miss teaching P.E., but I do miss the shape I was in."

"You could still get back in shape. You could start playing some of your sports again."

"Some of *my sports*?"

"Well, they're certainly not *my* sports," I told him with a laugh. "You know how I feel about organized athletic situations."

"Even if I didn't, the phrase 'organized athletic situations' would probably give it away."

I laughed again.

"So I do have some news," Dad added. "I am very close to signing a lease on a new place but I just have to figure some things out with my job first."

I felt a surge of excitement. *A new place!* I decided the moment had arrived. "That sounds great, Dad. I'm really sorry about what I said to Mel about us being here. Like I said, I don't really care that much about any of that." I was rambling, as usual. "The one thing that made me so upset was the fact that Aunt Pam is allergic to dogs. And I know you hadn't said yes to me having one at all yet. But . . . something happened, right after the fire. There's this dog. I know what you're going to say—*another* dog. But this one was—he *is*—different. Potato . . . his name is Potato. And I really, really wanted him to be my dog. But my friend . . . Lily, her family adopted him."

I wasn't trying, I swear, but a couple of tears slipped out.

"Oh, Cecilia. Why didn't you tell me about this . . . Potato?"

I wiped at my eyes. "I've asked for a dog before. A lot."

Dad frowned at me. "Not recently."

I thought back to my decision to put off asking my dad. Waiting for the Couch Monster to be less of a couch monster. Maybe if I'd been more honest with Dad about how I felt, I could have had a dog a long time ago.

But then, maybe, I never would have started volunteering at Orphan Paws, and then I never would've met Potato.

"I'm really sorry about this dog, C. But at least your friend adopted him." Dad hit himself in the forehead with his palm. "*That's* why you're always wanting to stay over there!"

"Yeah, that's a part of it."

"Well, I'm glad you still get to see him." Dad started for the door.

"Wait! I was going to ask you something."

Dad turned around with a knowing look. "You want a dog. When we move to our new place."

"Yes. I really do."

Dad sat back down beside me. "Okay. I'm going to say a *tentative* yes to a dog . . ."

"Oh my gosh!" I shrieked in his ear and hugged him again.

"I said *tentative*. There will be conditions. Honor roll. Possibly even your participation in at least one organized athletic situation."

"Ew," I said automatically, but when Dad started to shrug, as though to dissolve the deal, I added, "No! I'll do sports. I'll find one that I'm not horrible at. Maybe."

"Well, that's a solid plan. Now, I'm off to go for a run."

"Really? It's been"—I looked down at my watch—"about three years since you exercised."

"I know. But I have to start somewhere."

"Totally. Let's start with a long walk." I jumped up. "I don't have to go to the Chungs' yet. I'll go with you. If you want?"

Dad smiled again. "I want." He looped one arm through mine and then we spent the next half hour searching for his sneakers before heading out on our walk.

As we walked, another thought flickered into my head amid the happy ones about the heart-to-heart I just had with my dad.

If I am allowed to adopt a dog in the potential near future, could there be a way for that dog to be . . . Potato?

I knew it was crazy, but Eric had said that if Potato didn't earn his keep as a show dog, his parents might let him go. That would have been a bad thing when I *didn't* have the space for him in my home. But now I would. Or at least, I would soon.

Would it be wrong to botch a dog show for my own selfish gain?

Supplies for sabotage

1. Potato's favorite chicken cookies (a lot of them)

2. A conveniently placed table

3. A trusty accomplice

21

Awkward Music Express

A bunch of people showed up at the carnival, probably because there's not much to do in Winchester. There were food trucks, games, rides, and, of course, cotton candy.

Eric, Lily, and I walked onto the carnival grounds together. I was trying to look at Eric without being caught looking at Eric—to see how he felt about being stuck with me for the weekend. And also to see if he could sense that I was plotting to take his dog back.

It was just a matter of proving to the Chungs that Potato was not dog show material. I understood the point Eric was trying to make, but why did Potato have to be the one to suffer to make it? My plan was simple. I would sabotage the upcoming dog show, then volunteer to take the pesky, disobedient *rescued* dog off the Chungs' hands.

My scattered, evil thoughts led me to trip over a cord coming out of the funnel cake truck, and Eric had to grab my arm so I wouldn't go down.

I straightened up and tried not to think about the first time Eric had caught me, in the hall at school, when we kind of officially met. A lot had happened since then.

"There it is—COTTON CANDY!" Lily went rushing off toward the stand.

"I guess she really likes cotton candy," I said.

"She loves it," he said, not meeting my eyes.

"Yep."

"Cecilia?"

"Yeah?"

"Are you okay?"

I took a deep breath. I met his eyes. "I'm okay. Why?"

"You usually talk more."

"I'm just really hungry," I lied.

"Oh, okay. I'll go get us some funnel cakes," Eric offered. He went over to the truck window.

My stomach fluttered as I watched him walk toward me with two forks and the delicious, deep-fried confections. Were the flutters from guilt? Or something else entirely?

After Eric and I ate our funnel cakes, and Lily ate an entire bag of her favorite addiction, she asked, "You guys want to play some games? Or we could hit some rides."

"Rides!" I said quickly. My dad had always been suspicious about rides that were set up and torn down in new places all the time, so I hardly ever got to go on them.

"Okay, rides it is. You pick the first one," Lily said.

I turned in a circle and looked around. I spotted one in the distance that was turning the carts around in a fast circle and blasting music. It was pretty bad music, but it still looked like fun. "How about that one?"

We walked over to the ride, which was called "Music Express."

I figured I'd ride with Lily, since the cars were for two people, but then she ran into Emily in line with two of *her* friends.

"Oh, good—perfect!" Lily announced, turning to me and Eric. "You guys can ride together and I'll ride with Em."

Ack. I'd be riding with Eric.

We all handed in our tickets to the blasting sounds of an old nineties song, and Eric stood aside for me to pick which side of the little cart I wanted.

The ride started a few minutes later, and I realized my mistake. The ride went around and around very fast, squishing the person sitting on the outside seat—me—against the side of the person on the inside seat—Eric. I tried to sort of fight the awkward squishing, but after about three turns around, I gave up. You can't fight gravity.

When the ride finally came to a stop, I jerked back from Eric so fast it was like he had some sort of contagious disease.

I slid back onto my side and the ride operator pulled up the safety bar. My legs felt all rubbery from going around so fast, and from the stressful seat-smush.

"I wish you could forgive me," Eric said then, in a very low voice—so low I wasn't even sure I'd heard it.

And then we didn't speak again for the rest of the day.

The next morning Eric and I worked with Potato in the yard. We didn't speak to each other, and I wasn't sure if Eric noticed that I was giving Potato less encouragement than usual.

"So did you ask your dad if you can come to the regional show on Saturday?" Eric finally asked me, breaking the silence.

"Of course." I looked up at him. "A deal's a deal. I know I need to be there." I felt a jolt of worry, as if he knew I was planning something that would not only make him look foolish but also possibly ruin his reputation with both his parents and the greater dog-show community.

"Oh. I was just checking."

I looked back down. Potato was sitting between us and looking from one of us to the other, an inquisitive look in his big brown eyes.

"It starts at nine in the morning," Eric reminded me. "So maybe you could stay here on Friday so we can leave early."

"Maybe. I'll have to ask my dad." Then I remembered something else about that weekend. "But my best friend, Melody, will be visiting that weekend, too."

Eric shrugged. "Have her come to the dog show. I'm sure she can stay over here, too. My parents won't mind."

"Well, I'll see you at school, then." I bent down to pet Potato good-bye before heading into the house. He licked me all over my face before I reluctantly handed him back to Eric.

"I'll see you soon, P," I told Potato. "See ya, Eric," I added coolly.

For some reason I glanced back as I was heading up to the front of the house. Eric was just standing there, holding Potato, not moving at all.

22

Second thoughts about sabotage

"I just can't get over this new Cecilia Murray," Mel was saying for about the billionth time.

"I have one new friend and I went to one dance. Oh, and I got my hair cut. The amount of shock you are having over it is starting to become an embarrassment," I told her, readjusting Potato on Lily's floor so I could lie down flat on my stomach. He gave me a grumpy look for making him move before sighing loudly and lying back down beside me.

It was Friday evening—the day before the dog show—and Mel had come to Lily's house with me after school. It had been awesome to be reunited with Mel when she and her parents arrived yesterday. Her parents were even letting her stay with me—last night she'd slept on an air mattress in my borrowed room at Aunt Pam's, and we'd gotten *all* the parents' okays for her to sleep over with me at the Chungs' for the night before the dog show. I'd been a little nervous about having her hang out with Lily, in case the two of them didn't get along, but so far it had been going great.

"I'm not experiencing shock," Mel went on. "Just the appropriate amount of appreciation for the new you."

"Well, from both the old me *and* the new me, I suppose I'll try to have the appropriate amount of gratitude."

Lily stretched out between us and set a bowl of M&M's on the floor. She looked from me to Mel. "You two are so funny," she observed. "You talk the same."

"The big words are her fault," I said. "Mel's a genius."

The genius threw a pillow at me. "I'm not a genius." She laughed. "I just like learning. If you put the same effort into your schoolwork that you put into making all those lists, or volunteering at O.P. . . ."

"Ooh, what lists?" Lily asked.

Mel grinned. "Cecilia makes these really funny lists all the time. But she barely even shows them to me. They're all in this journal she keeps. You should start writing fiction, you know," Mel told me. "You could write a book!"

I blushed. "Nah. I'm not even in high school!"

"So? Taylor Swift got her first deal with a recording company when she was thirteen," Mel said.

I sighed. "Mel is obsessed with Taylor Swift," I told Lily.

"Me too!" Lily cried. "High five!" She and Mel slapped hands, and I couldn't help but laugh.

"I just admire how Taylor is so accomplished and goes after her goals," Mel explained.

"You know," Lily said, grabbing a handful of M&M's, "you sound sort of like my brother, Eric. I'd say the two of you should date, but maybe you're too similar. Besides, I kind of think he likes another girl." She smiled mysteriously.

My heart stopped, and Mel and I exchanged glances. Mel's theory, which she explained to me last night, was that despite everything, I had a crush on Eric Chung. And *that's* why I was so upset by what had happened at the dance. I'd blushed as I lay in bed and told Mel that she was wrong, of course. Wasn't she?

But who was Lily talking about? I knew it couldn't have been me.

Besides, once I carried out my get-Potato-back plan, it wouldn't matter what I really felt about Eric, or what he felt about me. I was pretty sure whatever non-friendship we had would be ruined.

"Eric's totally goal-oriented, too," Lily went on with a groan, grabbing more M&M's. "He *already* worries about his college applications. Not that he needs to. He's student council president and captain of the basketball team."

"That stuff seems like kind of a strange combination with dog shows," Mel observed.

"Well, he always liked animals," Lily told her. "There was one dog that he was particularly attached to: Porkchop. He was a naughty puppy, but Eric loved him the most. He was really sad when he died, and I think he channeled all that sadness into taking care of the rest of the dogs. You should see him with Potato," Lily added, looking over at me. "Sometimes I catch him in the dogs' room, singing to Potato, making up these silly songs to help him fall asleep. From what he's told me, Potato had a lot of trouble going to sleep when he first came to our house."

My heart swelled, and then sank. That was the cutest thing I'd ever heard. I wasn't the only one who sang to Potato? Eric did, too?

But then I strengthened my resolve. I was determined to get Potato back, and to end his dog-show career. Eric may have been sweet to Potato, but he still was only using him as a *tool* to *prove a point*. I just wanted Potato for Potato. So that made me more deserving. So my plan was fine. It was totally ethical.

Right?

Later that night, after Lily had fallen asleep, I filled Mel in on The Plan. I felt really guilty; Lily was a good friend of mine, but at the end of the day she was still Eric's twin. The Plan would have to be kept secret, between only me and Mel for now.

Both Mel and I were bleary-eyed when we had to wake up early to get ready for the show. Lily and Mel would be in the audience, so they got to dress casually, but since this show was a *formal event*, as Eric had explained, I had to wear something nice. So I'd selected a stiff green suit that I'd found in the depths of my cousin's closet—it was definitely *formal*. And best of all, it came with a matching jacket that was going to play a crucial role in The Plan.

When we met Eric downstairs, he was wearing his own black suit and white shirt and looked annoyingly good.

The regional show was being held at the big fancy hotel in the center of town. As Mrs. Chung drove to the show, I tried to act normal around Eric so he wouldn't be suspicious.

"Cecilia, why are you being so strange?" Eric asked me point-blank.

And here I'd been trying to act normal. This proved, once and for all, that I was a terrible actor.

"I'm fine," I lied, avoiding his eyes as we got out of the car. When he didn't say anything else, I snuck a look at him, and he was frowning at me.

"If you're nervous—"

"I'm not nervous," I broke in quickly, and he shrugged, looking hurt.

Keep your eyes on the prize, Cecilia, I told myself.

We walked into the ballroom where the show would take place. Lily and Mel went to take their seats in the audience, and Eric, Mrs. Chung, Potato, and I went into the "backstage" area, which was a huge conference room packed with tables and dogs and their frantic owners and trainers. Dogs barked, whined, and pranced, and trainers whistled, whispered, combed, fluffed, and paced. There was a buzz of nervous energy in the air.

Eric picked up Potato and put him on the small table we'd been assigned, where the little guy sat, looking from Eric to me. Eric's mom was a few feet away, talking on her cell phone. Officially we were here to "help" Mrs. Chung (even though she hadn't had anything to do with Potato's training). Potato looked anxious, even though I'd already whispered in his ear that today was going to be the end of his show business career, if I had anything to say about it.

I felt another flicker of guilt at all the hard work Eric and I had both put in to getting Potato ready for the show, but I shooed the feelings away. I had to focus on my endgame: Potato, resting on the couch next to me and my dad, in our new place.

Mrs. Chung came over to us. "You two ready? Our category

223

is next. Oh, I should say are you three ready?" She laughed and stroked Potato's head.

"He's ready," I said, picking him up.

Eric touched my shoulder. "Seriously, C. Are you super nervous or something?"

"Or something," I told him. I bit my lip and looked away.

We followed his mom into the ballroom. There was a huge circular space in the center for the dogs to run. It was just like the Winsted Winner's Circle, only much bigger and indoors. A small black-and-white dog was trotting around as we walked in. There were lots of people in the rows of metal folding seats. I caught sight of Lily and Mel and waved. Dad and Aunt Pam had also wanted to come, but Dad had had to go into the office for work, and Aunt Pam had a friend's baby shower to attend. I'd told them it was fine if they didn't come—in fact, it was better for me. I'd also been worried that Lori might come, but she'd called yesterday to say she'd be too busy at O.P.

We got to the starting area, and I had to give Potato to a lady in a peach-colored suit. She whipped out a little measuring tape and started checking him out thoroughly, making noises that I couldn't figure out. I honestly couldn't tell if he was passing or failing. They were being much more thorough than at the last show. She recorded all her mysterious results on a clipboard and handed him back to me.

"Excellent specimen," she pronounced.

"Thank you?" I responded. It really seemed like sort of a strange compliment. *Excellent specimen?* Potato was more than that. He was kindhearted and good and warm. But Potato still lifted his head regally, as if he knew he was being praised.

We stood waiting for a few more minutes while the current round finished, and then it was our turn. This show was arranged by breed. There were only four pugs. So my work was really going to be cut out for me, especially since I now knew what a great "specimen" my little Potato was.

We watched a dappled black pug make the circle. He seemed very young and puppyish, and he kept speeding up and slowing down. His owner or trainer, a big man in a tweed suit, kept frowning down at him.

We were up next. My stomach tightened. I was going to be the one to lead Potato around, just like last time. I smoothed down my green skirt. I'd had to assure Eric earlier that it had no pockets.

But my jacket did. And that was the key to The Plan. I carefully removed the green jacket and set it down on the table near the end of the ring. I knew just how cookie-motivated Potato was. The plan was to have Mel sneak over and stuff the jacket with Potato's favorite treats, then lead Potato within smelling distance of the jacket and let his chicken-cookie addiction take care of the rest.

But then I looked back at Eric. We locked eyes, and I saw the eagerness and hope in his expression. I felt a new wave of uncertainty wash over me. I thought about the songs Lily told me Eric sang to Potato, and the way Eric had always been nothing but kind to the little pup. I realized then that it was selfish of me to try to take back a dog that was never really mine to begin with. Potato already had a good home with someone who loved him. And regardless of what Eric anticipated, I knew Eric's parents would see it the same way.

And there was something else as well. I blushed as Eric's dark eyes held my gaze. I was starting to get the feeling that Mel was right. As much as I wanted to resent Eric, I couldn't deny I'd grown to like him. *Like him* like him. It wasn't just that he was cute—which he was. It was the way he and I had connected—about dogs, and *Star Trek*, and everything. And even though I knew he saw me as just a friend—potentially less—I couldn't let my hurt feelings get in the way of his dog-show/Potato dreams.

But before I could motion to stop Mel, out of the corner of my eye, I saw her sneak up. She was following the next phase of The Plan—to stuff dog biscuits into the jacket. I tried my best to steer Potato as far away from the jacket as possible, but I underestimated his smelling range. Even from across the room, Potato knew what was in that jacket, and he would stop at nothing to get at it. He bounded across the room with the force of a Great Dane, and I had no choice but to let him drag me.

As I'd predicted, Potato started jumping up to try to reach the treats. He wouldn't trot forward—he wouldn't do anything except jump up, hoping for chicken goodies. Eric looked at me in panic. Mrs. Chung was back on her phone and was missing everything. As much as I tried to steer Potato in the correct direction, he found a way to wriggle free from my grasp and run to the jacket, eventually succeeding in pulling it down. Then he managed to poke his nose in and get a mouthful of treats. He dragged the jacket with him over to me, then he started doing the circle like we'd practiced, only he had a mouthful of green jacket trailing behind him.

The lady in the peach suit came over to us and told me we had to stop and that we were disqualified.

Disqualified.

My stomach sank.

My plan had worked.

I scooped up Potato, suit jacket and all, and walked back over to Eric.

"What happened?" He was staring at me with his mouth open.

"I—I—I'm sorry," I stammered. I couldn't even bear to look him in the eye.

"Are we disqualified?" Eric asked.

I nodded, staring down. Potato was still in my arms, his head down now, as if he knew he'd done something wrong.

Eric went over and told his mom what had happened, and she shook her head, looking disappointed. Then he motioned for me to join him in the backstage area. Clutching Potato, I did so.

"Cecilia," Eric said quietly, "I saw Mel stuffing your jacket with treats. Were you *trying* to sabotage Potato's performance? I don't understand."

I looked up. Eric's expression was a mixture of disappointment, anger, and confusion.

I paused, debating telling him a lie. But then I realized it wasn't worth it. I let my words pour out. I told Eric everything—about my dad finally letting me have a dog, and my plot to make Potato fail so badly that he would lose the dog show, and then no one in the Chung family would want him. As I spoke, I felt terrible, but also like a weight was being lifted.

"But," I continued, looking seriously at Eric, "when I saw how much you seemed to want to win, and when I heard about what a good job you were doing taking care of Potato, I knew that I needed to put my selfishness and my . . . weird feelings behind me and let go of the idea of keeping Potato. But it was too late. And I ruined everything. I'm so, so sorry."

I buried my face in my hands.

"Weird feelings?" Eric asked. "What weird feelings?"

Darn it! I thought. Why did I have to mention the mess that is my emotional state? And also, really? *That* was the only thing he took away from my long-winded rant?

"Nothing," I said quickly. "I just meant—I mean," I stammered. *Just say it, Cecilia,* I told myself. What harm can come out of being a little less chelonian? Of being braver? Maybe it was time to step out of my hiding place and into the light.

My heart was pounding, and I took a deep breath.

"What is it, Cecilia?" Eric's eyes searched mine, confused but not angry.

"I just—I just don't know what I feel about you," I blurted. "I made all these assumptions about you before we even met—that you were a snob, that you were arrogant, that you—"

"Go on, Cecilia," Eric interrupted, rolling his eyes. Still, though, no anger. He even wore a half smile.

"And then we met, and you took away my Potato, and I got so, so upset. I hated you."

Potato's ears perked up at the sound of his name. He leaned in, as if listening intently.

"You made me this deal, and at first I was in it for the money—which I recently realized doesn't really matter, but that's a whole other story—and for the Potato time. But then I got to know you better. And I . . . I kind of liked the guy I got to know." My cheeks were very hot.

Eric's eyes widened. I could tell I was freaking him out. But I was almost done with what I had to say, so I barreled on.

"So what I'm trying to say is," I said, trying to keep my cool even though my heart was pounding even harder, "I *like* you, Eric. Despite every bone in my body telling me not to. Even though you adopted the one dog I love more than anything in this world. Even though you can make me mad more than anyone I know. And I know that you don't like me—you made that really clear at the Spring Bash. But I just wanted to tell you everything—to try to explain what I did. I guess I just hope that we can be friends." I heaved a big sigh. "Oh, and I promise not to sabotage Potato's showbiz career again. And I won't try to steal him or any of your dogs . . . from now on," I finished, wincing. I closed my eyes, bracing myself for confirmation that he hated me.

But when I peeked, all I saw was Eric looking back at me, a huge grin on his face.

"What's so funny?" I asked, annoyed. "Is my mortification that amusing to you?"

"No, not at all," Eric said, trying to suppress a laugh. "It's just . . . you are *so* wrong. About most things." He started stepping closer to me.

"Wrong?! Wrong how?" I felt ridiculous, and not just because I was practically yelling during the intermission of a dog show and also wearing a ridiculous green suit (and also holding a dog that, let's face it, still kind of looked like a potato, excellent specimen or not).

Eric stared at me but didn't say anything. It seemed that he was searching for the right words.

"Just spit it out, Chung!" I nearly shouted. "Argh! You make me . . ." My words trailed off.

He stepped even closer, until we were practically nose to nose. "What, Cecilia? I make you what?"

I was glad he'd called me by name just then, otherwise I'm pretty sure I might have forgotten it. I definitely forgot to breathe for a few seconds. I put Potato down and held on to his leash.

Still standing close to me, Eric said softly, "You don't know a thing about how I really feel." He paused and stared at me for a few more seconds. "It was never really about the dog show . . . or proving a point. I mean, it was—I do still love rescue dogs and am pretty bummed that Potato didn't win today—but those things weren't really that important to me. What really mattered to me was finding a way to spend more time with . . . you." He looked down, blushing a little, then back up again. "Not unlike the great lengths you went through to spend more time with Potato." He bent down to Potato and gave his head an affection-ate pat.

I gaped at Eric, waiting for him to continue.

"And all that stuff at the dance, I only said it because I was trying to act cool in front of those guys. I know it's a shock, but they don't actually even think dog shows are all that cool." He stood back up, leaning in close to me again.

"Well, *I* don't think dog shows are cool," I interjected. But I didn't say more—I had no idea how to respond to the other stuff he'd said. My pulse was racing.

Eric laughed again. "Well, I think that's fine. We don't always have to agree on everything."

There's that word *we* again.

"So what I'm *trying* to say," Eric continued, "is that I like you, too, Cecilia. A lot."

Oh my God.

"But . . . I'm just your sister's weird friend," I blurted.

"You are my sister's friend. And you are a little weird. But you're also my friend. And hopefully more."

He leaned even closer, and then he kissed me.

His lips were warm, and the warmth spread all the way down to my toes in a matter of seconds. He pulled away and smiled down at me. "Make sense?"

I nodded, still at a loss for words. He leaned forward and kissed me again, but we broke apart when we heard the sound of throats clearing.

I turned around—Lily and Mel were standing in the back-stage area, beaming at us. "I knew it! I told you, didn't I?" Mel was saying to Lily, and she was nodding and smiling.

Mel winked at me.

When I looked down at Potato, I could almost swear he did the same.

Unbelievable/ amazing

1. First kisses at regional dog shows

23

Potato's message

"Come on down, what do you say? Get your tickets for this May Day!" Lily called out to the cafeteria at large. It was after school, and we were stationed at our table, selling tickets to the school's May Day festival.

"Do you have to do it like that?" I asked her.

"Like what?" she asked.

"In that weird voice. And in rhyme."

"I love to rhyme—all the time—have some lime!"

"Wow, for someone who loves it so much you certainly are bad at it," I said, laughing.

"Hey, you're new to the student activities committee," Lily teased. "You need to watch and learn!"

I laughed, and then I looked at my watch and stood up. "Eek! I have to go."

"We just got here! And we signed up to work the table until four," she reminded me.

"I know, but can you please, please cover for me, Lil? Dad said he had some big surprise, and he made me promise to meet him by four fifteen. Pretty please?"

"Okay, go." Lily waved a pile of May Day tickets dismissively. "Besides, since Eric bought tickets for you guys on the first day, what do you care who else is going?"

I paused in putting on my coat, feeling my cheeks warm up. "He did? That's cool."

"Well, what do you expect?" Lily laughed. "Aren't you guys, like, together?"

"I'm not sure," I admitted. It had been a couple of weeks since the dog show, and the kiss, and I'd been spending nearly every day with Eric, and it had been awesome. "But," I added, "he hasn't actually asked me to May Day yet."

"Well, he bought the tickets—he probably just forgot the asking part. Boys can be sort of slow about stuff like that," Lily said, nodding knowingly toward Joey Lewis with an eye roll.

"I guess," I said, thinking I still had a lot to learn about boys. "See you later?"

"Later!" Lily said with a wave.

I ran down the front steps of the school, and ran most of the way to Orphan Paws, where Dad was picking me up.

He was waiting when I got there, parked right in front of the shelter. "You're late!" he called, but he was smiling. "Get in."

I climbed into the passenger side and pulled the door shut. "I'm here . . . what's the surprise?"

"Keep your hair on."

"What does that *mean*?" I asked him.

He rolled his eyes at me. "It means you'll find out when we get there." Dad cleared his throat. "While we drive . . . I've got some news."

"What is it?"

"Well, first—I won my case."

"Dad! That's amazing!" I reached across the seat to side-hug him. Of course the seat belt snapped me back instead because he had to hit the brakes right then. We both laughed, and I blew him a kiss. "Guess I'll hug you later."

"I'm pretty sure you will," he said. "There's more—after the verdict, I got a new job offer. A small firm in Winchester. It will mean a regular salary. Plus, I'll still get to work on cases I really care about."

"Congrats, Dad!" I felt a swell of pride and happiness.

"Thanks, C. I'm really excited." And for the first time in forever, he looked it.

"So where are we going? To see your new office?"

We were at a stoplight, and Dad looked over at me and smiled. "That'd be kind of a boring surprise for *you*, kid. Nah . . . actually . . . we're here."

Dad turned down a quiet, tree-lined street, and we came to a stop outside a small white-and-blue house.

"Is this . . . ?" I asked, afraid to hope.

He smiled. "To rent—at least at first. I finally signed the lease today. This was the place I was telling you about. It's all ours."

I felt a huge rush of joy. The house was perfect. "That's awesome!"

"You don't know the best part," Dad added with a grin. "I made sure to check with the owner. She's fine with cats and small dogs. I already paid the pet deposit."

"That's great," I said truthfully. And it was. But even though I'd been wanting a dog forever, in that moment I didn't really want *a* dog. I wanted a specific dog: Potato. But he still belonged to the Chungs, even after what had happened at the dog show.

"Oh, sweetie, I know you had your heart set on Potato. But we'll find you another great little guy. First, go on inside and check things out, yeah? Your aunt Pam is calling—she's probably lost." He held up his phone and turned away to answer it, but there was a glimmer of mischief in his expression that I couldn't quite figure out.

I walked across the lawn, feeling excited for my dad, but a little wistful, too.

When I opened the door, Eric was standing in the middle of the empty room. He was holding a huge potted cactus. "I brought you something," he said.

I smiled, remembering the cactus he had brought me the day he took Potato away from Orphan Paws. "Another one? Thank you," I said, reaching for the plant.

"I'm glad you like it," he said, moving closer. "But it's not really the cactus that I was talking about."

He moved aside and I saw that Potato was sitting behind him, wearing a little sign around his neck. My heart jumped. There were also about ten other pots with all sizes and colors of cactus arranged all around him. I knelt to read the message Eric had written on Potato's sign in silver metallic pen.

There were just two words:

MAY DAY?

I looked up at Eric, grinning and blushing. So he'd just been waiting for a special way to ask me! "Yes, of course I'll go with you!" I exclaimed. I was glad my dad was still outside because I couldn't resist giving Eric a big hug and a quick kiss. He grinned.

"I'm glad," he said. "I already got us the tickets. Oh, and there's more. Look on the back of the sign."

I flipped the card over, and there were two more words:

I'M YOURS.

My heart melted. "Eric, that's so sweet," I said.

He blushed. "I mean, it's true. But see, that note is from someone else, too. It's also from Potato."

"What do you mean?" I asked slowly, not wanting to get my hopes up too high.

"Your dad said you are allowed to have a pet here. So, now . . . you have a pet here."

I hugged him so hard we fell over, and then we knocked over at least one of the cacti. Luckily the floor was tiled, but I probably wouldn't have cared either way just then. Potato came bounding up to us and I hugged him and cried on his fur, but this time they were happy tears. When I'd calmed down from the rush of joy, I looked up at Eric.

"Are you sure? I can't ask you to do that . . ." I realized in that moment it was too much to ask for him to give up his pet.

"You're not *asking*, C. I told you, Potato is yours. You two have always belonged together. Besides, I expect to have extensive visiting privileges."

"Of course!"

Eric reached over to scratch Potato's ears. "Also, he's got zero future in show business," he said, confirming what I'd known from the very start.

I couldn't help but laugh. "Thanks to me. And a pocketful of cookies." I looked down at the happy little dog in my lap. He'd taught me so much. Because he was brave enough to trust people, after everything that had happened to him, somehow I'd started to be just a little bit brave, too. I looked at the boy who sat beside me. And if it hadn't been for Potato, I'd never have known how wonderful Eric was.

"I have to admit, that was pretty brilliant of you with the cookies," Eric was saying.

"I hope your mom forgives me."

Eric smiled. "She likes you. She thinks you keep me on my toes."

"Thanks?" I said.

"That's what you said when I gave you the cactus. The first one."

I smiled. "About that. So I know I said no flowers. But . . . why did you choose a cactus?"

"I just thought . . . they're sort of like flowers, but . . . pricklier."

"The perfect plant for me," I said drily.

Eric pulled me toward him. "Exactly. My little cactus."

He kissed me, and when we pulled apart, Potato was looking from one of us to the other in that knowing way of his.

Just then my aunt Pam walked in and saw me sitting on the floor with a boy in a pile of cacti and dirt, with a happy dog bouncing around between us.

"Honestly, Cecilia," she said, shaking her head.

It was a full minute before I managed to stop laughing.